DREAM
PHAZE

Table of Contents

DREAM PHAZE

Germination

Book 1

Matt Watters

Red Giant Publishing
Australia

Book One: Paperback ISBN 978-0-9578199-5-5
Book One: Paperback first published 2022 by
Red Giant Publishing
Sydney, Australia
Dream Phaze Trademark owned by Matthew S. Watters

Chapter One

Twilight was ending as night beat day and engulfed the barren landscape. They gingerly entered the water.

'It's stinging my legs, Saxon. What's that smell?'

'Sulphur. Under no circumstances should we dive, splash, or put our faces into the water,' Saxon instructed. 'Unusual tactile sensation; it's sort of thick and soupy. What's your pain threshold on?'

'I'm on three,' Kris said.

'Me too,' Wendy confirmed. 'I shouldn't have shaved my legs this morning.'

'Don't go in too far, you might have trouble putting your feet back down on the bottom.'

The three of them lolled in the dense Dead Sea water, looking up at the burgeoning night sky. Small foam bean pillows supported their heads.

'So, besides the floating sensation, stinging cuts, and the danger of swallowing this muck, what are we doing here, Saxon?'

'Relax, Kris, enjoy the experience for a moment, we have time. Notice there are very few sounds here.' Saxon heard someone entering the water behind him but didn't look back.

'Hello, Saxon.'

He instantly recognised her voice. 'Evening, Lena,' he smiled.

'Hi, Lena,' Wendy chimed in.

'Lovely night for a dip.' Lena waded into the water beside Saxon and reclined.

'Look up there,' Kris pointed at a faint glow in the eastern quadrant of the night sky. 'Meteoroid?' The radiance grew in intensity, then an abrupt flash exploded into flares rippling out like fireworks.

'Exploding meteoroid,' Wendy agreed, watching tens of thousands of shooting stars pepper the heavens. 'Spectacular!'

'Wow, it's beautiful,' Lena whispered, as the sound wave touched them with a faint crack.

'About 13,000 years ago, just north of this region,' Saxon explained, 'early nomadic tribes, hunter gatherers, began staying put in the one place. They collected plants, animal meat and skins, and settled down around their larder to became hunter collectors.'

The others bobbed, mesmerised by the light show above as they listened to Saxon's lecture-style storytelling.

'At that time, a sizable meteoroid entered the atmosphere and exploded into a massive meteorite storm covering almost a third of the planet.'

'So, we're going to have meteorites rain down on us?' Wendy asked.

'One theory goes, this event changed the planet forever,' Saxon continued. 'It helped initiate a 1300-year cold period that wiped out the megafauna across North America. Tonight, we will be re-testing the–'

'Involuntary death exit protocol,' Kris finished.

'Correct.'

'I don't know, Saxon,' Wendy was concerned. 'Being hit by a meteorite is not my idea of entertainment.'

'C'mon, we might feel a little pain, but look at this, it's a visual feast.'

The meteorite shower blazed across the night sky, mirrored on the water, sandwiching the group in an array of light. Tens of thousands of projectiles were pulled by gravity at supersonic speeds, echoing crackles as they neared. Chunks of rock hurtled past them hitting the water and fizzing, exploding.

'This is getting scary,' Wendy said. 'Sounds like a battlefield.'

'It's fucking awe–' Kris started.

Salt water washed over Saxon the instant he heard the explosive thwack from the missile that smashed Kris.

'Shit!' Wendy screamed. 'One's taken off my leg and it stings like a bitch.'

'Don't exit early, Wendy!' Saxon's eyes, nose and mouth burned as space debris pelted the now churning, bubbling water.

'I–' A meteorite decapitated Wendy.

Through blurred vision, Saxon barely saw the two rocks that violently tore through his body, severing him in half. He stayed aware for a fleeting moment.

Brain and body functions on every level were being monitored by a multitude of technologies crammed around the three sleep pods. The assistant worked feverishly checking, rechecking each member of the team.

Kris returned first. 'That was one of the best yet,' he said groggily. 'They back yet, Merlin?'

Merlin hovered over Wendy checking the device in his hand. 'Alpha blocking activity, adrenaline levels high, heart rate up, blood pressure up, not good.'

Kris immediately hopped off his sleep pod and went to help.

'Maybe...' Merlin reached to counteract her adrenaline level.

Kris gently gripped his hand. 'Here she comes.' They watched as Wendy came around.

'What's happening?' Saxon stayed on his sleep pod rubbing his eyes.

'Wendy's testing us again,' Kris replied.

'All good,' Merlin reassured them.

Wendy opened her eyes. 'That was intense.'

'It was fucking awesome. Excellent job, Saxon.'

'I aim to please, Kris.' Saxon removed his forearm dashboard and earstims before sitting up. 'Debrief in 30 minutes.'

Saxon stood at one end of the meeting room scrolling through projected holographic data visualisation diagrams, before opening a functioning brain recording. Wendy and Kris arrived and stood around the projection. 'Where's Merlin?'

'Coming,' Wendy said.

'How are you feeling?' Saxon questioned.

'Fine. Hungry, but fine.'

'Me too,' Merlin added as he entered the room. 'All the data's downloaded and ready.'

'Thanks, Merlin.' Saxon tapped the menu to restart the recording. 'All the neurotransmissions initiated by Synmem code were released as planned and we all exited as anticipated.' The Dynamic Emission Neuroimaging recording of Wendy's brain displayed millions of colourful spikes firing throughout her brain. 'There was one small glitch with you, Wendy, here.' He paused the DEN recording, enlarged an area with his fingers and pointed. 'Increased calcium interrupted synapse, specifically these synaptic vesicles being received by receptors, but that delay was eventually compensated for by adrenaline to increase gap junction coupling.'

'I'll have a look at that after lunch, shouldn't be an issue in future,' Kris assured them. Kris tapped a file to bring up a data visualisation set. 'The immersion entry data was all perfect, as was our spatial perception, sensory engagement and group consciousness integration matrix.'

'Any issues with the platform or network, Merlin?'

'Dream Immersion Platform and Norus are humming along. The neurometric ancilloscope still isn't calibrating correctly, I'm running a self-diagnostic and update as we speak.'

'Good. Thanks, everyone,' Saxon praised. 'I'm pleased the involuntary death exit protocols are now working as per our new simulations. Well done.' Saxon was a solid framed man, fit, in his mid-40's and an achiever, a high achiever. He expected the same standards from his team.

'Have you been modifying the spatial perception data, Saxon?' Wendy asked. 'That experience felt different to even the last immersion.'

'It's improving with each experience. I've been testing new sequences with exteroceptive and interoceptive neurotransmission processes in the occipital lobe and pons. Haptic spontaneity more precisely, it seems to be working.'

'I don't want to give too much away, but I'm working on tasting fire,' Kris announced with a wicked grin.

'That sounds utterly blistering!' Merlin yelled. 'Can I go, Saxon, pleeease?'

'Can't wait for that one, but for now I'll settle for chilli beef balls and soba noodles,' Wendy confessed. 'Who's in?'

'I'm in!' Merlin's chunky shape reflected his predilection for overindulging.

Wendy laughed. 'That's a given, I meant, Saxon and Kris.'

'You know I can't help it, it's my Greek DNA.'

Alfred Nembo came in wearing his typically aloof expression, his PA and a young woman followed. 'Good morning,' he paused, then looked his watch. 'Good afternoon, Dr Setri, Dr Kilroy, Mr Tripidakis. We need to talk, Saxon.'

'We do?'

'We do.'

'I'll catch up with you.' The others took the hint to leave. 'Let's sit down, Alfred. How are you, Mrs Freudenstein?'

'Fine thank you, Dr Zynn,' the thin, angular woman replied, starting the recording app on her personal device. 'This is Zen, our new office intern.'

'Hello, Zen.'

The petite girl smiled.

'Zynn and Zen.' Alfred's mouth curled at one side of his plump face.

'What can I help you with, Alfred?' Saxon asked straight faced.

'Walt is concerned we will not meet the deadline for the launch.'

'I told you 12 months ago, Alfred, we'll need more time.'

'It is not you and your team he is concerned about, Saxon, it is the regulator. They require more data before they will sign off.'

'Regarding what?'

'Notification of completion for phase II clinical trials at all sites was submitted last month, and as you know, the data revealed there were no issues. Now they require more data on thalpherycine residue dissipation in the 24-hour cycle before they grant the licence. Do we have that data available?'

'They know after testing thalpherycine for three years, it is totally organic. It's basically in our biochemistry as acetylcholine.'

'That may be so, but without the required data we do not move forward.'

'I don't understand their rationale, they know it's biosoftware. It limits norepinephrine, serotonin, and histamine production during immersion to induce muscle paralysis; it mimics the process of natural dreaming–' Saxon was cut off.

'That is part of the purpose. It also reacts with Synmem code to create neurochemical sequencing. We need that data to move to the final sign-off of clinical trials–'

'But it's inert without Synmem code present, it dissipates naturally.'

'But as it could be used daily, they require more data confirming thalpherycine residue dissipation after Synmem code activation before we can move forward.'

'You didn't say that, you said–' he glanced at Mrs Freudenstein with frustration.

'Dr Zynn, we are in the final stages, if they refuse approval all this will be for naught. The first regulatory authority to approve is always the hardest. Other regulators will fall into place if we can get it over the line with the first one. You know how it works, Saxon.'

'It'll take a day to pull it all together.'

'Good, thank you. That will keep the program on schedule. We have a very tight strategic timeline.'

'How is beta testing progressing?'

'Beyond our expectations. Very positive feedback. The clash between marketing and branding is over and they have agreed on a name for the product launch, "The Event". It will be released simultaneously worldwide across all media platforms. Hardware distribution network stakeholders have signed on. Dream pod production is on track, and licensing agreements for Dreamplexes are in final draft. Fifty million dream immersion devices are in production for the first quarter, with a further 60 million for the second quarter. The hardware infrastructure centre for managing the network platform is almost complete, with capacity to deliver uninterrupted coverage to half billion users simultaneously in stage one. Manufacturing of the Gatekeeper of Dreams authoring units is well under way.'

'Those numbers seem to have grown, Alfred.'

'They have. Based on testing feedback over the last month our sales and marketing projections have boosted production by 30 percent. We estimate early adoption will be swift and significant.'

'I hope so, to justify those numbers.'

'Saxon, the Tremaine Group has always believed in you, from proof of concept through to commercialisation. Walt and the board have invested considerable capital in Zynn Communications. We are now in the global entertainment industry and the Dream Immersion Platform is a world first product; entertainment will never be the same once it is released.'

Saxon contemplated Alfred's response for a long moment before turning to Zen. 'How old are you, Zen?'

Zen looked at Alfred and Mrs Freudenstein, then back at Saxon a little surprised. 'I'm 20, Doctor.'

Merlin stood working at the diagnostic terminal, deep in concentration, as Zen exited the elevator to the lab. She cleared her throat as she descended the stairs.

Merlin spun around, 'Hi.' He maintained eye contact, his pupils dilating. 'Zen?'

'I'm, I'm not sure why I'm here. Mr Nembo sent me to help. What do I have to do?'

'Not much really. Sit here and I'll talk you through the procedure.'

'Procedure?' Her head tilted as she sat on a stool.

Wendy entered the lab and trotted down the steps. 'Don't scare the girl, Merlin.'

Merlin laughed nervously. 'Sorry, it's not a procedure. Wrong word, I mean the process we use for dream immersion.'

'Merlin, like the wizard?'

'It's Melvin actually, but we call him Merlin. Wizard with electronics he is,' Wendy grinned. She watched the two of them for a moment, the biochemistry between them clear.

'Does it hurt?'

'Does what hurt?' Merlin asked vaguely.

Zen offered a mischievous smirk. 'The process.'

'Erm, no, no, it won't hurt at all.' He showed Zen the earstims then placed one in his own ear then removed it. 'The earstims work in synergy with this to deliver frequencies.' Merlin placed the device around her forearm. 'This is the dream immersion or DI dashboard; both are parts of the DI platform which connects to the network. The DI dashboard is where you'd enter your experience preferences.'

'You have crumbs in your beard,' Zen informed him.

Merlin awkwardly brushed the crumbs from his manicured beard. 'Gone?'

'Yes. Why are you testing this on me?'

'Saxon mentioned you were 20 and we both thought it would be a good opportunity to test the age restriction access protocols for the platform. We've developed an algorithm that restricts anyone under the age of 21 from accessing dream immersion, as a safety precaution.'

'So, nothing will happen to me today because of my age?'

'Exactly, so you have nothing to worry about.'

Saxon arrived. 'Morning, Zen, thanks for agreeing to help us out. As you know, this project is highly classified, so we need people we can trust.'

'Melvin, I mean Merlin said it probably won't work on me.'

'Correct, that's what we expect to happen, which means our safety protocol works. We've run the simulation hundreds of times, the more data we collect the better.'

Wendy checked Zen's DI dashboard. 'What year were you born, Zen?'

'2027. I love your hair. Is it naturally that red?'

'For 32 years, since I was born. Okay, in a minute I'll give you a thalpherycine wafer, put it on your tongue and it'll quickly dissolve.'

'What does it do?'

'The thalpherycine wafer works on two levels. It makes you sleep and it's a vital part of the DI platform, it contains the catalytic agent for Synmem code to create the dream immersion experience.'

'But I thought I wasn't going to–'

'We have to go through the process as if you were 21, Zen,' Saxon interrupted. 'You won't be denied access until the cell analysis is completed. You'll be asleep during this process, but not in dream immersion.'

Wendy continued. 'Just after you start sleeping, your cell age will be analysed and you'll be denied access. You'll wake up a few minutes later.' Wendy offered Zen a thalpherycine wafer and pointed to her mouth.

'Please come over here, Zen,' Merlin instructed. 'Lay down on the sleep pod.' Merlin placed a monitoring sensor on her finger.

Wendy walked over to Saxon and whispered. 'Which experience will I program for her? As this is our first clinical test since the upgrade, if the protocol doesn't work–'

'It'll work, but if it doesn't–'

'Something I've been working on?' The redhead suggested along with an encouraging smile. 'It's age appropriate.'

'Sure, why not.'

Five minutes later, Merlin called Saxon and Wendy back into the lab.

'Look at this. Zen's in dream immersion.'

'The protocol failed,' Wendy assumed.

'Nope, look at her cell age analysis,' Merlin pointed to the readout.

'7,696 days, she's 21 years one month,' Saxon said quietly. 'Who's got their PD? Mine's on my desk.'

'Mine too,' Wendy said.

'Where's your PD, Merlin?' Saxon asked.

'Erm, you know I don't use it during work.'

'Bullshit,' Saxon said sternly.

Merlin offered a guilty look before he pulled his personal device from his back pocket.

'Open the IAM app. Open her right eyelid, Wendy.'

Merlin held his PD above her face as the Identity Access Management app took biometric scans of her iris and face. 'Her stored info says she's 20 years and two months.'

'Get security in here, Merlin.'

'Should I wake her?' Merlin queried.

'No. She's not going anywhere, more data the better. The cell analysis certainly worked, just not in the way we expected,' Saxon said heading back to the developer's lab.

Zen stared at a mesmerising spectrum of light that danced on a turquoise lake, before realising the origin of the colours, a colossal rainbow overhead. A festival of people a short distance away beckoned her with music and peppermint floating on the zephyr. She strode along the dirt road with euphoric excitement, a rare feeling she thought. Zen admired the spectacular purple and red forest of flowering jacaranda and flame trees on the far-off hillside. Finally she reached the celebration, the place where the rainbow touched down.

'Welcome. Can I tempt you with a flavour?' the man asked Zen.

'A flavour?'

The man pointed to the rainbow. 'We have blueberry, passionfruit, peppermint, strawberry, orange, mulberry and plum.'

'I have no money.'

'It only costs a thank you and a smile.'

Zen thought for a moment. 'I'm not sure.'

'How about a portion of each?'

'Erm...' her lips pursed momentarily. 'Okay.'

The man scooped down an exaggerated helping of each flavour into an oversized double cone. 'You'd better hurry up; the skytrain is about to leave.'

'The skytrain? What skytrain?'

'The skytrain over the rainbow of course.' He nodded towards the futuristic transportation hovering 100 metres away.

Zen took the cone and tasted. 'Mmm–gelato. Thank you.' Zen strolled to the skytrain licking her confectionary. She found a seat as the skytrain departed, slowly ascending into the sky.

Twenty-five minutes later, Merlin went to the doorway of the developer's lab. 'Zen's waking up, security is here too.'

Security guards and Mrs Freudenstein waited with Alfred Nembo as Saxon and Wendy entered the lab. 'What do you know about her, Alfred?'

He deflected the question. 'Mrs Freudenstein?'

'Not much, she came through our usual security screening channel, Jetstone Personnel. They are usually an extremely diligent organisation.'

Zen woke to the group standing around her, staring.

'How do you feel, Zen?' Merlin asked.

She considered the group. 'Okay. I thought I wasn't supposed to dream?'

'Sit up please, Zen.' Saxon's demeanour was authoritative.

Zen sat up, removed the earstims and gave them to Merlin. 'Why did I dream?'

'You told me you were 20 years old.'

'Yes.'

'That's not true, is it, Zen?'

'Yes, no, maybe not,' she stammered. 'Ohhhh...sorry! My brother thought my birthday was 13th of June 2027. It's been years since we...discussed if my records were actually correct.'

'You entered dream immersion. Cell analysis recorded your age at 21 years, one month,' Saxon told her. 'Born July 13th, 2026.'

'That could be right. I was born in Vietnam, they found me living on the streets of Hanoi with my older brother. We were separated, and I grew up in an orphanage until I was five, so there certainly could be a mistake in my birthday. Sorry,' she cringed.

Alfred glanced at Saxon before speaking. 'We need to confirm those details, Zen. Come with us please.' Alfred gestured to the security guards and they moved towards Zen.

Zen removed the DI dashboard from her forearm and handed it to Merlin with a smile. 'For what it's worth, Dr Zynn, that was one of the most exhilarating experiences I have ever had, thank you. It was so realistic.'

'Wendy created that one,' Saxon admitted.

'Thank you, Wendy.'

'I've called it Tasting Rainbows.'

'I did, I tasted rainbows, yay!'

Her tiny figure was dwarfed by the burly security guards, as the group watched her being escorted from the lab.

'Can I have a quick word, Saxon?' Alfred requested.

Saxon gestured to his office.

Mrs Freudenstein followed them with PD in hand, recording.

'If this turns out to be an issue, we may have to isolate Zen until after the launch,' he confided.

Saxon considered Alfred and Mrs Freudenstein for a long moment weighing up what that actually meant, knowing Alfred's history for getting things done. 'Agreed.'

'By the way, I have been told McTavish down in research has made a breakthrough with project Rapid Sun. He will be presenting his report at the Friday meeting.'

'We should proceed with extreme caution, Alfred. Delivering entertainment is one thing, recording an individual's memories for law enforcement is–'

'You know that is not the primary application for memory preservation, this is a by-product, a financially attractive by-product admittedly. I will see you Friday.'

Alfred and Mrs Freudenstein left Saxon feeling uneasy.

Saxon sat in his office momentarily daydreaming, looking down but seeing up, the reflection of his ceiling fan refracted in his water glass. Saxon was known for contemplating life from a unique perspective. He had always been curious. The gangly teen started his first university degree in Australia aged 16. Saxon had a rare gift for understanding complex math and physics, no doubt inherited from his father, George

Zynn, a respected scientist who commercialised his own technology into a global business.

Saxon resumed checking his mail, deleting as he went. He opened one that caught his eye. He read an excerpt from a decade old story on the Science Now news site, dated 10th August 2036.

'The Maiquetia Conference 2036 was convened to define a set of guidelines for an emerging technology—human memory preservation. Around 304 scientists, as well as academics, reporters, and ethicists gathered at the Aqua Luna Hotel conference centre in Venezuela.

Sources reported a more stimulating conversation, over Screwdrivers in Professor Amanda Voss' room on the fourth floor of the hotel, discussing dream manipulation.

Professor of Biomedical Engineering at the University of Oxford, Amanda Voss, is a staunch opponent of dream manipulation technology. Her Oxford colleague, Professor of Neurochemistry, Saxon Zynn, the proponent of Dream Immersion technology, the theory dubbed by NeoScience Magazine as the holy grail of dreaming, clearly champions dream exploration.

Discussions were impassioned between the eight key individuals in room 424 until sunrise, but still the two Oxford heavyweights were at diametrically opposed ends of the argument. Asked for a comment, Professor Zynn told Science Now, 'Dreaming is a reality to be experienced.' He explained, 'We exist on more than one plane, in our waking moments and in our dreams. Both are different manifestations of reality.'

The Venezuelan conference reached little consensus, as privatised, economic self-interest got in the way of open discussions about the risks and benefits associated with specific uses of the technology.'

'A decade on and you've created ZynnComm and Amanda married Jeremy Abernathy! Best wishes, Scarlett.'

Saxon knew the sender, 'scarlett.drummond@cs.ox.ac.uk', another ex-colleague from his Oxford days. He saw someone out the corner of his eye, Merlin and Zen were heading towards the developer's lab. Saxon wandered out.

'Hi, Zen. Alfred informs me everything has been sorted out.'

'It has, Dr Zynn. Jetstone did a further background check and I'm okay to stay. Thumbs up! I've wasted months when I could have been getting into pubs and clubs a lot earlier! Damn!'

Saxon laughed. 'I'm sorry we were all a bit, dramatic the other day, but we have to take security very seriously, there's a lot at stake for this project.'

'I completely understand, Dr Zynn. It was a wonderful experience, I'm very intrigued by it all.'

'I'm going to show Zen how we author dreams,' Merlin explained, eager to keep moving.

Saxon smiled at them, before he returned to his mail.

The pair entered the small developer's lab where several men were working at one end.

'So, this is where the magic happens?'

'Not magic, extremely intuitive tech. This is part of it, there's a much larger developer's lab on level three. This is the DI platform engine, the Gatekeeper of Dreams.' A squat black octagonal prism sat on the bench. Merlin handed Zen a pair of glasses. 'Put these on.' He put his glasses on and touched the side of the computer, initialising the augmented interface projected in space in front of them. 'The dreamforming interface allows developers to create environments, weather, atmosphere, soundscapes, vehicles, people, beings, anything down to the finest detail with the tools menu. The realms of possibility don't apply to the Dream Immersion Platform; if you can imagine it, we can author it.' He selected a cityscape from the menu and dragged it into the conception space. 'You can customise attributes individually or let the program render it automatically, but then it becomes truly intuitive.' He instructed the computer to render the landscape in vivid colours. 'We've developed innovative machine learning using accelerated predictive-adaptive response software within the environment, for every action there's a reaction in real time–'

'I don't have a clue what you just said, but it sounds impressive.'

'Sorry, I don't get to tell too many people about what we do, I got carried away,' Merlin confessed.

'Do you write code for the Gatekeeper computer?'

'The four of us write Frequency Hypgenic source code, but codesters like those over there do most of it,' he pointed to the three at the other end of the lab. 'FH code creates the tools and content for the dreamforming interface. We have teams of codesters creating stock libraries, along with catalogues of specific experiences: rally driving on Mars, time travel experiences past and future, extreme sports, and dozens of interactive games.' Merlin trashed the cityscape and brought up a new project. 'Using audio and video recordings, we can digitise anyone into experiences too. We can create an imaginary friend or alien.' He enlarged a furry six-legged beast. 'This is my mate Skip. He–'

'How long can you stay in dream immersion?'

'Thirty-three minutes total. That's one of the DI laws.'

'Laws for dream immersion? Is the age restriction a DI law? Are there others?'

'There are about ten, they're still working on them. But I think the coolest feature of DI is group consciousness in any experience, being physically present in the same setting with your friends even if they're halfway around the world. That'll be the backbone of the platform, massive multiplayer interactive experiences offering unprecedented reality that can be saved and continued experience after experience–'

'Can you get hurt in dream immersion?'

'Did you feel anything in your experience?'

'Yes! I could taste, smell, all the senses were there. It was no different to being here now. It was totally twisted.'

'You can certainly feel pain in immersion. That's another law, if you die you automatically exit DI. There's a series of sensory level preferences on the DI dashboard, no pain at all through to feeling everything. You have a personal transparency level too, you can be translucent or solid, or anywhere in between, and that in turn triggers gravity thresholds, no gravity to full gravity. Gravity is hard to control–'

'I could be virtually invisible and float like a ghost–'

'Yes, but you have very little control over how you move when you lose body mass and float.'

'Are there disjointed, odd, random dreams, like our normal dreams?'

Merlin stopped and looked across at her.

'What?'

'You can have those dreams any night you sleep. Why recreate something you do naturally? Dream immersion is about authoring immersive, structured, customised entertainment experiences.'

'Of course.'

Merlin continued without missing a beat. 'Once the experience is authored and rendered it's translated through a BASE neural compiler into Synmem code, or synaptic memory neural code. The experience is downloaded to the DI dashboard from the network and delivered via inaudible frequencies through the earstims which spark neurotransmitter chemical messages in the thalamus and–' the thump on the floor took his attention.

Zen lay crumpled on the floor, blood pooling around her head.

Wendy stood at the doorway to the lab. 'Merlin, I need help. We need to keep going with the algorithm for–' She paused when she saw Merlin kneeling over Zen.

'Wendy!' He shouted.

'What happened?' She checked for a pulse.

'She must have hit her head as she fell on the side of the bench.'

The codesters were now watching. One of them handed Wendy his PD. She tapped the medical alert app and positioned the device on Zen's cheek. 'Is she diabetic?'

'I don't know.'

'Scanning. No vital signs detected,' the app voice reported. 'Paramedics alerted, ETA eight minutes. Automatic resuscitation system required. Automatic external defibrillator required.'

'Get both pieces of equipment, and Saxon!' Merlin yelled at the codesters. 'Should we give her adrenaline?' he asked Wendy.

'I'm not sure. It could do more harm than good,' Wendy warned as she removed the PD and rolled Zen onto her back to attach the auto CPR device. 'Get a bandage for her wound,' she directed a codester.

Merlin held the PD against Zen's face.

'Delta brainwaves diminishing. No electrical function detected,' the device advised.

Nine minutes later the paramedics arrived. 'Is she responding?'

'Nothing, no pulse or breathing. We've used the AED four times,' Saxon explained.

One of the paramedics attached a monitor. No vital signs. 'We'll try Epinephrine.'

'I wasn't sure if we should administer adrenaline,' Wendy said.

'Best you waited,' the other paramedic said as he injected Zen.

Zen remained unresponsive after 20 seconds.

'She's gone,' the same paramedic announced.

Saxon closed his eyes, sighing.

'There's absolutely nothing you can do?' Merlin insisted of the paramedics.

'It's been almost 12 minutes and there's no activity. She's gone. I'm sorry.'

'Fuck! Come on, please!' The tears disappeared into his beard.

Saxon turned to Merlin and gently shook his head. 'She's gone, buddy.'

A prolonged silence settled in the room.

'Why did this happen, Saxon?' Merlin wore the tragedy on his face.

'I don't know, Merlin, maybe I shouldn't have–'

'Shouldn't have what?' Merlin asked.

'Asked her to volunteer,' Saxon replied in a quiet voice.

'This isn't your fault, Saxon, or yours, Merlin,' Wendy reassured them.

'Epic fail,' Merlin muttered.

Putting an arm around Merlin, Wendy walked him slowly out of the lab, her cheeks damp with grief.

Chapter Two

The compact, transparent craft skimmed at speed several metres above the ocean surface towards the fast-approaching, massive neon blue swell. The craft gently climbed to clear the peak of the thirty-metre roller and descended the other side. Merlin eased the joystick to the left to stay in front of the next even larger wave in the impressive set. Merlin maintained the craft a metre off the surface of the gigantic swell, before he flicked the joystick quickly to the left for an unexpected barrel roll.

'Whoooa! This is fucking amazing!' Zen squealed.

Merlin positioned the craft on the shoulder before dropping down the face as the wave began to break perfectly over them, forming an enormous shimmering blue tube, a hollow that a container ship could ride. Merlin manoeuvred the craft up into the pocket to avoid the deadly impact zone of the crashing lip, then slowed to become immersed inside the liquid tunnel. He held the position inside the roaring hole for what seemed like an eternity. The setting sun kissed the horizon, a point Merlin now aimed for. He accelerated, emerging from the glassy barrel to shoot up over the shoulder of the wave to head out for another ride.

Kris and Wendy patiently waited for Merlin to return.

'I hope he enjoys the experience,' Wendy said. 'He's been so depressed the last few days.'

'Seeing anyone die is devastating, let alone someone you're sweet on.'

'The entire world looks different when you're infatuated. How old's Merlin?

'Hmm,' Kris thought. 'Twenty-seven I think. No...26.'

'The counselling should help.'

'As will this. Here he comes,' Kris announced.

Merlin stirred before opening his eyes.

'How was it?' Wendy asked.

'Blew the haircut off my head!' He removed his earstims, then his DI dashboard. 'The codesters did such a good job.'

Saxon, with his wife Margo, Walter Tremaine, the chairman of the Tremaine Group, and his EA, James, exited the elevator into the lab.

'Margo!' Wendy yelled, rushing to hug her.

'It's wonderful to see you, Wendy,' Margo responded with an equally enthusiastic embrace. 'Hello, boys.' She greeted Kris and Merlin over Wendy's shoulder.

'Morning,' Kris welcomed. Merlin just nodded.

'How are you, Kris? Wendy?' Walt Tremaine asked, not expecting a response. He walked over to Merlin who was still sitting on the sleep pod. 'How are you, Merlin?' Walt's age was etched in his face.

'Fair to average. I've just returned from an elevated echo test with Zen.'

'What's an elevated echo test?' Walt asked.

'There are four main categories of characters so far in dream immersion experiences, we've called them echoes,' Wendy explained. 'Live echoes are our customers, living users. Elevated echoes are deceased people authored for specific experiences, like Zen. Assembled echoes are the extras in every experience, created from scratch and populate all environments at all times. There are also host echoes, which can be living, elevated or assembled characters. Hosts can be active across multiple experiences. For example, a host might be created in the image of a living celebrity who hosts a sporting event.'

'Lena's an elevated echo,' Kris added. 'The same as Zen.'

'How was it?' Saxon asked Merlin.

'The codesters used all the facility recordings of Zen and I boosted her sense8 performance with the expanded vectigon metrics. Now she looks and sounds exactly like her.'

'We thought it would be good for morale to keep Zen around for some of our experiences,' Saxon explained to Walt.

'Great idea. It was a sad state of affairs, I'm sorry it happened here.'

'Considering her condition, it could've happened anywhere,' Kris said, adjusting his metal rimmed glasses. 'She wasn't even aware of her congenital heart disease looking at her medical history. She would've been dead before she hit the ground, it was that fast.'

'For her maybe,' Merlin quipped. 'Not for us.'

Walt put his hand on Merlin's shoulder. 'You know, my father always said we were just bubbles on the breeze; some lives are briefer than others. Death is the inevitable consequence of living, Merlin. I've lived a long time, I'm a tough old bubble, and time has a way of putting everything into perspective,' the silver haired man imparted. 'That terrible sense of loss wedged in your heart will fade.'

Melancholy thoughts grappled with the silence for a moment.

'We'll see her in dream immersion,' Saxon assured Merlin.

'How's Hugo, Margo?' Wendy asked, changing the conversation.

'The boy needs to apply himself,' Walt spoke up.

'Oh, Dad! He's 20 and in his first year at university. He is applying himself.' Margo grabbed Wendy's arm and dragged her towards Saxon's office. 'Let's catch up.' The women walked off.

'We'd better keep moving, Walt, we'll be late for the meeting,' Saxon prompted. 'We'll catch up after lunch, Kris.'

'Push the meeting back an hour, James,' Walt instructed his EA. 'I want to have a go.'

'Yes sir.' James took out his PD.

Saxon glanced at Kris and Merlin. 'A go? You mean dream immersion?'

'Yep. About time I experienced what all the fuss was about.'

'But, the department heads are waiting, Walt,' Saxon stressed.

Walt stared at Saxon for a moment. 'Who's the major shareholder, Saxon?'

Saxon smiled. 'You are, Walt.'

'Let 'em fuckin' wait.'

'You heard the man, Kris, let's give him a ride.'

Walt watched James tap his PD. 'While you've got your phone out, I mean PD.' He looked at Saxon. 'Remember when they were just a phone and a few apps?'

'Just,' Saxon said.

'Get a photo of us. Come on, Merlin, Kris,' Walt gestured to Saxon.

'Ready?' James took the photo.

Merlin walked over to James. 'I'll have a copy of that thanks, Jimmy.' Merlin held his PD against James' and James swiped the image across.

'Not for publication on any platform until we publish,' Walt reminded Merlin.

'Of course sir.'

'What type of experience would you like, Walt?' Kris asked.

'Got anything historical?'

'Dead Sea Lights?' Kris suggested to Saxon.

Saxon gave Kris an annoyed look. 'No. The codesters have just finished Battle at Edessa, Persia 260 AD for our history catalogue.'

'Romans? Sounds like fun.'

'Spectator or participant?' Kris enquired.

'Participant? I'm a bit old to participate in a Roman battle, I'll observe, Kris. Coming, Saxon?'

'Sure, why not.'

'In costume or as you are?' Kris asked.

'Walt?' Saxon prompted.

'Which uniform, Roman or Persian? Can we go in neutral clothing?'

'Of course, Arab thobe, like a robe,' Kris said.

'I know what a damn thobe is, Kris. Done.'

Walt and Saxon straddled their horses surveying the belligerent armies across the bleak plain. Roman foot soldiers were being fired upon with volleys of arrows from thousands of Persians archers.

Saxon watched as Walt patted his horse, and then smelt his fingers.

Walt dismounted. 'I feel 65 again. I haven't ridden in decades,' Walt declared.

'You're pain threshold is on two,' Saxon told him.

'I wish I had a pain threshold in the real world that I could dial down,' he chuckled as he squatted on the ground. Scooping up a handful of dirt, he let it run through his fingers. A smile ran across his face as he gazed up at Saxon. 'I can smell the horse, feel the breeze on my face, feel the texture of the dirt with my fingers. How the hell did you manage to create all this in such detail, Saxon?'

'I can't accept kudos for it. You know this was a team effort, Walt.'

'Of course, but the knowledge behind the technology is you, Saxon.'

Saxon smiled, pleased with himself. He had waited patiently for this moment; the moment Walt was curious enough to fully embrace and appreciate his son-in-law's technology. 'Thank you, Walt. It took tedious, meticulous work over many years. I remember about 13 years ago when I first told you about my idea for dream immersion, you said to me, "Why do you get to interpret what dreams are and what they represent?" That really rang true to me. Why me? What did I have to offer? You made me examine the project more seriously, dig deeper, tease out the essence of what I was searching to create. For all the code that made it into the final program, there were days, weeks, months of code discarded, regurgitated, tested, before any results emerged. It's not luck, or divine guidance, or genius. It is weeks, months, years of trial and error, of challenging work.'

'I take my hat off to you, Saxon, this is phenomenal. You've created something remarkable.' Walt stood beside his horse as he saw a rider approach in the distance.

'Why did you wait so long to experience dream immersion?' Saxon asked.

'Seemed like the right time and place to do it. From the very early prototype, I've always believed you could achieve what you set out to do. Alfred showed me the beta testing feedback–extraordinary! So, I thought I'd better try it for myself. I remember when early VR was commercially released in the early 1990s, then the evolution of online massive multi-player gaming, then the re-emergence of VR with online gaming and simulated environments. Now all the buzz is location based VRXLR8 complexes with extended realities. But this, this is...it's like an alternate living reality, so much beyond anything I imagined. It is fully immersive, fully interactive, non-invasive, and it's portable! Every adult on the planet will want to experience it.'

A woman rode up. 'Hello, Saxon.'

'Hi, Lena. Remember Walt?'

Lena, brunette and tanned, stared at Walt for a moment. 'Of course I remember, Margo's father. Hello, Walt.'

Walt smiled at the young woman. 'Hello, Lena, good to see you again.' He turned to Saxon. 'This is mindboggling, Saxon; you've created revolutionary tech.'

'Dad always said he was the smart one in our family,' Lena declared.

'George and Amanda would be proud of you, Saxon,' Walt agreed.

'C'mon, we're wasting time, let's get closer,' Saxon insisted. 'Do you need a leg up, Walt?'

'No! I feel fantastic, I think I'll be right.'

The three riders trotted towards the warring hordes, then halted to watch. The Persian cavalry in full battle armour, both man and beast, surged full bore into the advancing Roman legionnaires. The air reeked of blood and spilt body fluids as their horses ventured closer, stopping a hundred metres from the fringes of the battlefield. The trio watched hungry vultures rip the flesh from bones of mutilated soldiers.

'Egyptian vultures,' Walt explained. 'The Roman Emperor, Valerian, marched his 70,000-strong army eastward to the Sassanid borders. His forces included almost every part of the Roman Empire, including Germanic troops, but they were thoroughly defeated then captured by the Persian King, Shapur the First. Shapur had a very well-trained cavalry, and only half the number of men as Valerian. One of the most decisive victories of the Roman-Persian wars. That fellow over there looks like he could be a leader.'

King Shapur in full military regalia, surrounded by guards, sat rigid on his stead as a prisoner was brought forward. Shapur glanced across at the battle tourists and pointed. A party of soldiers broke away and rode towards them, surrounding them. A Persian officer slowly circled.

'King Shapur requests your presence,' the officer ordered.

'This is getting interesting,' Walt commented with a grin.

The group was escorted to King Shapur.

King Shapur pointed to the prisoner. 'Do you know who this man is?'

The tourists looked at each other.

'Valerian?' Walt offered.

'Get off your horses,' King Shapur commanded.

Soldiers gestured to them to dismount. They were made to kneel beside Valerian. King Shapur signalled to an aid and Valerian was dragged over to his horse.

'Get on your hands and knees like the dog that you are,' King Shapur instructed Valerian. King Shapur stepped onto Valerian's back, then to the ground. 'Why do you wear such attire?' King Shapur demanded of Saxon.

'We are travellers from across the sea.'

'How can we understand them?' Walt whispered to Saxon.

'Language preferences in the DI dashboard. I set ours to English.'

Walt pulled at the sleeve of his thobe uncovering his wrist, expecting to see the DI dashboard. A green digital time display sat on his skin, counting down.

King Shapur grabbed Walt's arm. 'What is this?'

'A new way to measure the day,' Saxon replied quickly.

'Give it to me.'

Saxon peered at Walt through troubled eyes. 'It's on his skin, he can't take it off.'

'I can. Sever his arm!' King Shapur ordered.

'Wait!' Saxon protested as soldiers stood Walt up. 'Take mine.' Saxon stood and pushed Walt out of the way. 'Look, I have one too.'

King Shapur glanced across at Lena. 'Take the woman to my tent.' Two soldiers grabbed Lena and dragged her away.

'Saxon!'

'Six minutes left,' Walt said.

'You'll be all right, Lena, trust me.' Saxon turned to Walt as soldiers prepared to remove his arm. 'This is one of those times when we have to cut and run, Walt.' The soldier raised his blade. 'Remember the safe word?'

'Jabberwocky,' Walt recited. A red aura briefly shimmered around him before he dematerialised.

'Jabberwocky,' Saxon repeated as the razor-sharp sword sliced through his arm, causing a momentary sting before he vanished.

Thirty minutes later, Saxon and Walt were in the meeting.

'So, onto to new business. Walt.' Alfred introduced.

'Thanks, Alfred.' Walt stood and paced slowly around the polished timber boardroom table. 'You all know how the Tremaine Group began; we cut our teeth on commercial wind farms and solar electricity, moved into electric and hydrogen powered vehicles and aircraft, real estate, mining, etcetera. Some say our glory days are long gone,' he paused. 'Late last week we were made aware of a disturbing series of events that will impact the entire Tremaine Group, all the companies under our corporate umbrella. Jackson Briggs, now ex-CFO of the parent company, concealed the fact from our board that the Carmine partnership deal fell through, a 23 billion dollar investment. He concealed this for two months, while telling the board all was on track. We had already leveraged that investment and borrowed against it for our Eringa Red Project in China. As a result, Briggs has been charged with fraud by the Shanghai stock exchange regulator. Forensic auditors are combing over everything in our Shanghai, Sydney and New York offices as we speak. The Tremaine Group has been fined 28 million dollars for non-disclosure and non-compliance.'

Murmurs rippled around the boardroom. Saxon threw a worried look at Margo, but her sculpted face evaded his gaze. He knew Margo was concerned as she fidgeted with her manicured fingernails.

'What does that mean for ZynnComm, Walt?' Alfred asked.

'I'll get to that, Alfred. Needless to say, the Eringa Project is on hold, indefinitely.' He stopped pacing. 'Staff at one of our casinos, the Iridium in Moscow, have been caught allegedly manipulating gaming machines, accused of laundering large sums of money, and involvement in illegal drug transactions. The Kremlin wants to close the Iridium and our four other casinos across Russia. We're expecting both pieces of information will be made public sometime today. A devastating blow for the corporation. We'll be in damage control, and I'm flying to Sydney after this meeting for the anticipated media frenzy.'

More discussion erupted around the room as Walt continued his walk.

'This morning before I arrived at the facility, I had the weight of the planets on my shoulders ladies and gentlemen—until I experienced the future.' Walt continued, now fixated on Saxon, 'Dr Saxon Zynn, our dream master, will revive the Tremaine Group with our Dream Immersion Platform and Gatekeeper of Dreams authoring technology.

We will return to our glory days. Our testing feedback, along with my personal experience this morning, is telling me, nay shouting at me, we are going to transform entertainment as we know it. We are on the verge of a massive entertainment revolution that will fuel public imagination. Everyone will want what we are selling!'

Spontaneous cheers and applause erupted around the room. Saxon glanced at Margo, who was no longer playing with her fingernails, instead wearing her beguiling *proud of you* smile.

That evening, Saxon and Margo relaxed under the transparent dome above their residence. They were immersed in the star-packed night sky. The only on-site abode sat on level one of the underground ZynnComm facility, located six kilometres west of Port Augusta, South Australia. The small city in the middle of nowhere was known as the Crossroads of Australia for rail and road between the north, east, west, and south. It was also readily accessible via air and sea.

A year of scoping, analysis and preparation had gone into the selection of the secure location and establishment of the facility. Smart domes doted the 140 hectares of flat, uninspired land. They doubled as solar collectors and agriculture biospheres providing unlimited power and basic food resources for the eight underground levels of the facility.

Beside Margo and Saxon's surface dome, a large hangar housed aircraft and maintenance, a reception office, and the elevators to lower levels. A staff car park was tacked on to the other end.

Margo's PD buzzed in her hand. 'It's Hugo.' A hologram of Hugo Zynn's head projected from the device. 'Hello darling,' she said.

'Hiya, Mum.'

Saxon put down his device as Margo moved closer. 'How are you, buddy?'

'Can't complain for a young fella. I need to ask you guys something.'

'Sounds ominous,' Saxon cautioned, looking at Margo.

'I could tell you a few of the boys are going to Hawaii for a week to surf at the end of exams and I want to go with them, but that wouldn't be true. I want to go to Hawaii, but I want to get married there.'

'What! To who?' His mother demanded.

'Christine of course–'

'You've only been going out for a few months, Hugo!'

'Seven months actually, Mum. That's a month longer than you two before you got married.'

'Have I met her?' Saxon whispered to Margo out the side of his mouth.

'Yes!' She snapped.

'You're okay with it then?' Hugo seemed pleased.

'Not yes to you! Yes to your father!' Margo was annoyed with both of them. 'Say something to your son, Saxon!'

'How are your exams going?'

'Are you fucking serious!' Margo scolded Saxon. 'You're not getting married, Hugo, you're barely 20!'

'Settle down, Margo,' Saxon asserted. 'This is Christine Knox we're talking about, right? Her father's the dentist?'

'Yeah, she came over for dinner last month when you were here.'

'Do you love her, Hugo?'

'I think so, Dad.'

'Well buddy, you have to know so. You're going to be spending the rest of your life with this girl–'

'Nobody gets married at 20 these days, Hugo!' Margo interrupted. 'Are any of your friends married?' Margo questioned, knowing the answer.

'No, but you were 21 and Dad was 22 when you got married,' he reminded her.

'It was different back then. Wait until I get back to Sydney and we'll discuss this,' she negotiated.

'When are you back?'

'I'll be back in Sydney Friday.'

'We'll be in Hawaii by then and we want you and Dad to fly over for the wedding.'

'Why get married in Hawaii and why so quick?' Saxon asked.

'Chris is from Hawaii remember, she's American, and I really like the place. My boys will be there and–'

'You are not getting married, and certainly not in Hawaii! You should be concentrating on your exams.'

'I've only got one more tomorrow and that's it for this semester.'

'We can't just drop everything and fly to Hawaii, Hugo.'

'I can,' Saxon volunteered. 'Kris can look after...' Margo's death stare stopped him in his tracks.

'He is not getting married and we are not going to Hawaii!' Margo firmly enforced.

The trio fell silent as Saxon's PD buzzed. 'It's Walt.'

'I saw Pop on a news feed this afternoon,' Hugo commented. 'Everything okay?' A bell chimed Hugo's end. 'There's someone at the gate, hang on.' Hugo answered the intercom. 'Yes?' Mumbles were heard.

Walt's head glimmered in the night sky from Saxon's device. 'Have you seen the news?' he bellowed.

'No comment,' Hugo told the person on the intercom.

'Is everything okay?' Margo asked.

'Media sniffing around. Is something going on?'

'All hell's breaking loose!' Walt exclaimed.

'We have to go. Make sure you answer when I call later, Hugo.' Margo disconnected.

'Did you hear that? Media at our Sydney gate,' Saxon informed Walt.

'It's not the Tremaine story, it's the fucking ZynnComm story,' Walt explained.

'What are you talking about?' Margo quizzed.

'We have more problems on our hands, we have a stranger in the house. Our meeting this morning was leaked. You've been dubbed the dream master, Saxon, and the story's gone viral.'

'Shit,' Saxon said quietly. 'Does Alfred know?'

'He told me.'

Margo opened a news feed on her PD. The ZynnComm story came up first.

'How the fuck did it leak?' Saxon asked.

'Who knows? Alfred's got security on it.'

'That room is certified ASO C5. Nothing can penetrate it,' Saxon pondered aloud.

Margo noticed a brighter light in the night sky heading towards them.

'You need to lay low for a week or two at the facility,' Walt recommended.

'We can't. Hugo wants us to fly to Hawaii, he says he's getting married!' Margo said.

'Married?' Walt was taken aback. 'I told you that boy couldn't apply himself.'

'Bloody hell, Dad!' Margo chided.

'I'll set up a meeting for tomorrow.' Walt disconnected, irritated at being reproached.

A sizable drone flew in low over their residence.

'That's a media drone,' Margo said as she tapped her device to opaque the dome of their residence. 'It's started.'

'Better get back on to Hugo and warn him.'

Chapter Three

'Get your grubby hands off her you fucking parasite,' Saxon said with distaste.

The filthy cowboy dropped Lena's arm and took a step back, his hand poised on his peacemaker. 'What did you call me?'

'You heard me.'

In a breath, the cowboy drew his six-shooter with his finger on the trigger, but Saxon was faster. His shot shattered the cowboy's right cheek and exited the back of his head in the blink of an eye. The cowboy's twitching body thumped the dusty saloon floorboards. Saxon holstered his Colt .45.

'Yeehah!' Zen screamed.

'Nice shot, Saxon,' Kris congratulated as the piano player started up again.

'Thanks, brother,' Lena said, giving him a peck on the cheek.

'Who's buying?' Saxon asked, leaning on the bar.

'You saved me, so it must be me,' Lena said.

Kris and Saxon were decked out in authentic 1860's American cowboy attire, while Lena and Zen were dressed as exotic dancehall girls.

'Pity Wendy didn't come along,' Kris commented, before knocking back a shot of whisky.

'You know she doesn't like this type of experience, not her idea of entertainment. Besides, this is a boys' own adventure.' Saxon downed his shot.

'Ain't that the truth!' Kris agreed. 'Bartender! Another round.'

At that moment, three raggedy cowboys burst through the saloon swing doors. They spied the dead man on the floor and walked over to him.

'Which one of you fucking coyotes killed Sweet Cheeks?'

The piano player stopped.

'Sweet Cheeks. Really?' Saxon whispered to Kris.

Kris shrugged. 'Keeps it light.'

Zen piped up and pointed at Saxon. 'He did.'

Saxon turned slowly around from the bar. 'Who are you?'

'Blossom Guts Gilroy.'

Saxon looked to Kris with a wide grin. 'You've had fun with this one.'

'Who are you?' Blossom Guts asked.

'Saxon the Destroyer.'

'Never heard of ya. Why'd ya kill Sweet Cheeks?'

'He was bothering my sister.'

Blossom Guts eyeballed Saxon as he walked over to the bar and lent on it. The long pause added tension to the already nervous saloon atmosphere. 'The boys and me don't like you, mister.'

'You'd better get out of Deadbury if you know what's good for you, Blossom Guts,' Kris warned.

'Who the fuck are you?'

'I'm your worst nightmare, Blossom. I'm the sheriff.'

Another member of the trio walked to the opposite side of the saloon. 'I collect sheriff badges,' he said, opening his waist coat to show off a dozen badges.

Kris whipped out his revolver and shot the man through the jugular. Blood gushed from beneath the cowboy's hand as he tried to stem the bleeding.

Blossom Guts stood bolt upright from the bar pulling his gun.

Saxon blasted him in the centre of the chest, propelling him backwards.

The last thug lunged at Zen and grabbed her around the neck from behind. He pointed his gun to her head.

'The hand eye targeting algorithm works like a charm,' Saxon commented.

'I think we need to dial it down, on a scale of one to ten. It seems a bit too easy.'

'Agreed.'

'Left eye.' Kris squeezed off a round into the left eye socket of the last cowboy standing, saving Zen. The piano player started up again.

'The cycle, the damn pay cycle,' Merlin moaned. 'Flush at the beginning and skint at the end, and then it starts again, 26 times a year. I'm rekt.'

'What do you spend your money on out here in the middle of nowhere?' Wendy asked.

'Good food and beer, online VR gaming, virtual clubbing, holoflix...'

'Do you save any?'

'Nah. That's what superannuation's for.'

They watched as Margo entered the lab from the elevator and headed straight to Saxon's office without even a glance towards them, leaving when she realised Saxon wasn't there.

'He's in dream immersion, Margo,' Wendy told her.

Margo walked down the steps and over to the sleep pod where Saxon lay. She stared at him for a long moment.

Wendy wandered across to her. 'Are you okay, Margo?'

'How long to go?'

'About six minutes,' Merlin said.

'We saw the media reports last night. Saxon said it was business as usual,' Wendy explained. 'Do you want to–'

'Tell him I want to see him,' Margo instructed, before turning and returning to the elevator.

Merlin shrugged at a confused Wendy.

Saxon left the lab and took the elevator to his residence on level one. Margo was working on her tablet as he walked in. The room was open plan, spacious and minimalist, except for photos of Hugo scattered around the room. One entire wall displayed a 3D outdoor vista; the apartment opened on to a green plain of gently rolling hills. The kitchen sat on the opposite wall, a single doorway at the far end led to three bedrooms each with an ensuite.

'I can't reach Hugo, he's gone offline.'

'Last night he agreed to wait until this media storm blew over,' Saxon confirmed as he sat beside her.

'That's what he said. I've tried his friends, including Christine. No one is answering.'

'The meeting is at eleven, we have ten minutes.'

'I know, I know,' Margo responded. 'He did this when he disappeared to Mexico. Remember?'

'Of course I remember.' Saxon and Margo flew to Mexico on that occasion to find their 17-year-old son. They eventually found him passed out by a pool in a luxury villa with two older women, all of them naked. 'Maybe he's still in the exam.'

Margo thought for a moment. 'Oh yeah, he mentioned that last night. I forgot all about that until now.'

Saxon took her hand in his. 'He said he would wait, I trust him. He's matured since the Mexico stunt.'

'I suppose so, darling, but he worries me.' She gave him a half-hearted smile. 'ZynnComm is trending everywhere, it's gone ballistic, positive and negative responses, much more positive though. This could be a blessing.'

'I'm not looking. I want to know how it was leaked. We set-up this facility in isolation primarily based on security. Fat lot of good that did if we've been infiltrated from within. C'mon, let's get to the meeting and we'll call Hugo after.'

Walt Tremaine was projected into the room from Sydney. Alfred Nembo and Margo sat with Saxon in his office.

'This facility was established in Australia because it's a stable democratic country, has a reputable, educated workforce and world-class infrastructure,' Walt explained. 'Security was one of the main concerns for the project. We chose Port Augusta because of the isolation and its reliable, unlimited power. Then this shit happens. It's just not good enough.'

'No, it is not, Walt. The investigation will find the source,' Alfred said. 'But if we do not launch early off the back of this publicity we will lose market advantage—' Alfred was cut off.

'There is no market advantage, Alfred, there is no market!' Saxon said in frustration. 'We keep going around in circles.'

'We still think there's no similar tech out there?' Walt challenged.

Saxon sighed. 'No. From our intelligence there doesn't seem to be.'

'Do we take that chance?' Walt continued. 'We were informed this morning the fucking Russian government is closing our casinos. That, coupled with our fine in China and the Eringa Red project being shelved, is a massive hit to our bottom line.'

'None of us saw this coming, Saxon,' Alfred offered. 'We have to adapt and keep moving forward. I suggest we accelerate the project with a soft launch in limited territories in one month, followed by global release in all territories in four months, in time for Christmas. The Australian regulator will approve our thalpherycine licence within the month. The rest will sign-off under the New York-Munich Biosoftware Convention. The hardware can be fast tracked, and initial feedback from the soft launch on social media will fuel the hype for the major release. We can distribute our own libraries first and hold back the Gatekeeper of Dreams authoring unit until the new year.'

'Is that achievable, Saxon?' Walt asked.

Saxon sat silent for what seemed like minutes. Everyone waited for his response. Responsibility sat heavily upon his face as he wiped sweat from his top lip. His decision would either propel the project at breakneck speed or keep it on the existing timeline. 'We still have months of testing but...possibly. We'll have to cut a few corners, increase content production, but we'll have the bare bones ready for a limited soft launch.'

'You may not want to hear this, darling, but there are benefits from this unexpected situation. The media gaze has shifted away from Tremaine Group issues and focused on ZynnComm. We can feed this media storm and whip it up into a hurricane of public anticipation. The speculation on social media is nothing short of phenomenal. ZynnComm is trending worldwide; we can't buy this sort of publicity,' Margo added.

'Okay,' Walt sighed. 'Then it's agreed. I know this isn't how you wanted the project to play out, Saxon, but I agree with Alfred and Margo, we need to move quickly on this and bring the release forward. Alfred, ramp up all unit production, and Margo, instruct PR to organise a few controlled leaks through the usual channels. We need to capitalise on this.' He turned back to Alfred. 'Tell Chen from security I want his report on yesterday's meeting by tomorrow.'

'Yes, Walt,' Alfred answered.

'Saxon, you need to light a fire under your content teams.'

'Will do.'

'Have you decided on the name for our retail distribution division?' Walt asked.

'Lucid,' Saxon answered.

'That was my choice too,' Walt concurred. 'The two of you need to stay put for the next week or so while marketing leaks the imminent product launch,' he suggested to Saxon and Margo. 'Ah, and Margo, we're going with Gerber Global Advertising as our exclusive partner for product placement in experiences. Your negotiating and recommendation was spot on, thank you.'

'GGA will be very lucrative for ZynnComm,' Margo assured them.

'Users still have the final choice if they want advertising, correct?' Saxon asked Margo.

'Of course. Ad free experiences will attract a slightly higher premium.'

'Since the leak we have had enquiries from the US Department of Defense, Boeing and the Royal College of Surgeons asking how our technology can be utilised for training. We need to accelerate the Dream Stream division to capitalise on business and government contracts. If Margo's team can leverage the leak to launch The Event across the globe, we have a clear-cut advantage,' Alfred added.

Thoughts danced frantically through Saxon's mind now that he had committed. Did his team have enough time? What if there was an unforeseen critical mistake? What if all the work scheduled for the next eight months couldn't be crammed into four? What if...?

'What's happening with Hugo?' Walt asked.

Margo and Saxon's eyes briefly met before Margo answered. 'He's agreed to put his plans on hold.'

'Good to hear the boy has come to his senses.' A voice off camera informed Walt he had another appointment. 'I have to get moving, we'll talk later in the week.' Walt disconnected.

'You need to meet with Veejay to finalise end user information.' Alfred stood. 'Things are going to move very quickly from here, Saxon,' he forewarned before he left the office.

Saxon wore a fixed stare.

Margo reached out and rested her hand on his. 'Now your baby is about to go out into the world. You have to let it go, darling.'

'You don't feel that way about Hugo.'

She squeezed his hand. 'That's different, he's our only child.'

'He has to leave eventually, and you have to let him go.'

'I know, but it's so hard.' She studied her fingernails.

'Yes, it is. This accelerated release worries me.'

'Everyone loves the platform, darling, it will be sensational,' Margo consoled. 'I'll try our first baby again,' Margo tapped her device. 'Call Hugo.'

'The person you are calling is not available, please leave a message,' the synthesized voice said.

Later that afternoon, Saxon and Veejay Kandy, the ZynnComm Actuary Manager, sat around a table above Saxon's residence. Overhead, gentle rain from dreary overcast weather splattered the transparent dome.

'Our risk assessment falls into three categories,' Veejay used his fingers to count as he continued. 'Number one, and most important, risk to users. Second, risk to our Norus network being compromised, and third, risk from content developers trying to disable protocols on the Gatekeeper of Dreams units. Users and developers will be given clear guidelines and warnings upfront, along with a disclaimer covering us. In regard to the network, we've run simulations on the highest risk probabilities and–'

'Let me stop you there, Veejay. Black Shield has less than .05 percent likelihood of being breached, so Norus has little chance of being compromised. As soon as any unauthorised external network access is detected, all hell will break loose. Our intrusion prevention system will kick in, blocking the user, followed by our search and destroy protocols. Norus master administrators use multilayered access authentication, so Black Shield has to be–'

'That's two administrators to login?'

'We've increased it to three,' Saxon boasted.

'Even better.'

'We hold three individuals' biometric scans of both hands and face. Their voices are authenticated when they input their unique alphanumeric code. Only one other person and I know the names of those individuals.'

'My team has identified probable breaches related to content authoring as it stands now. That's the best we can do without monitoring the units, and we can't do—'

'Remember, the CPU in each unit has a unique quantum identifier so we can trace breaches from here or the unit. Once the Gatekeeper of Dreams is released, experiences of every type imaginable will be authored,' Saxon explained. 'We already have companies lined up to create private networks to deliver them. Sex and violence will be part of that mix. I think with the limitations we've built into the system; we highlight the warnings in the end user license agreement.'

Veejay considered Saxon before answering. 'When was the last time you actually read a EULA? No one ever reads the fucking things; they just tick the box to say they have. We need every developer and user to be fully aware before they use our technology. That was one of the key issues raised by external watchdogs and consultants.' Veejay let out a heavy sigh. 'The reason we need to be so vigilant goes back to the implant tech trend a decade ago, to bioware. Remember the repercussions the Gambaldi incident triggered? The embedded tech industry virtually disappeared overnight, no one trusted it, they still don't. We don't want that to happen to us.'

'The Gambaldi incident was the reason I focused on non-invasive tech for dream immersion,' Saxon confided.

'Exactly, so we need, no, must have strong upfront warnings for users and content developers regarding risk, with the finer points in the EULA.'

'Are you talking about risk to the user or ZynnComm?'

'Both. There are risks and there are risks. Unacceptable risk comes into play on two fronts. The first is the dark nature of weird fucking individuals and groups using the tech for unintended purposes. The other front is safeguarding ZynnComm. We are putting people to sleep, taking them on a journey so life-like it's indiscernible from reality and back again in just over half an hour. It's about how our tech impacts someone from a medical, social, ethical, and psychological perspective. All it will take for ZynnComm to come under scrutiny is one vulnerable individual who is wired differently to die. There will be unforeseen situations and consequences, we can't predict or anticipate all scenarios, and that's why it's imperative to include upfront disclaimers and warnings, to limit the scope of rights users may exercise. I really would've liked the extra months to explore more vulnerabilities of the tech.'

'You and me both, Veejay, but there are other forces at play and bigger fish in the food chain.'

'I've taken up enough of your time,' he glanced at the time on his device. 'Our risk assessments are sufficient until we start getting feedback from real world use. I think our upfront guidelines and warnings are strong and I'll work with legal to go through the fine print,' Veejay concluded as he closed his device and gathered paperwork.

'I'll scrutinise the guidelines and warnings, and we'll meet next week to set them in concrete.'

'I've got to get a move on, flying to Melbourne for my daughter's wedding.'

'Which daughter, May or April?' Saxon asked.

'April.'

'How old's April now?

'Twenty-four. She has grown into a very well-rounded person.'

'You're biased,' Saxon smiled. 'Go, go get your flight. You don't want to be late. Good luck with the wedding, Veejay, and thank you.'

'No problems, Saxon.'

Saxon read through the draft version of the guidelines and warnings once more.

Disclaimer: Use the Dream Immersion Platform at your own risk.

By using our products and services you accept this end user license agreement ("EULA") and take full responsibility for making this decision. By using our products and services you understand that this is a legally binding instrument and agree to be bound by the terms and conditions herein. As the end user, you release Zynn Communications (ZynnComm) from all responsibility and liability associated with the use of the Dream Immersion Platform including all products and services associated with it. If you have a pre-existing medical or psychological condition, consult your medical professional before use.

1. *The Dream Immersion Platform is for mature participants only. Access is denied to users under 21 years of age.*
2. *Access is denied to intoxicated users.*
3. *Fluid intake should be limited prior to dream immersion and bladder emptied before entering dream immersion.*
4. *Users are limited to one dream immersion experience per 24 hours.*
5. *Dream immersion experiences are a fixed period of 33 minutes. Entry into and exit from dream immersion will be a maximum of four minutes for each.*
6. *Dream immersion experiences can be remembered or erased. This choice must be made prior to dream immersion.*
7. *Dream immersion experiences can be for an individual or within a group environment. This choice must be made prior to dream immersion.*
8. *Dream immersion experiences can be a Once only Experience (OoE), a Series of Experiences (SoE) or a Continuing Experience (CE). This choice must be made prior to dream*

immersion.

9. *The Dream Immersion Platform offers the choice of a kill switch or safeword for immediate exit from experiences. This choice must be made prior to dream immersion.*

10. *The Dream Immersion Platform offers a built-in safety protocol (Involuntarily Exit) if death is experienced during dream immersion.*

THIRD-PARTY GENERATED CONTENT WARNING: Extreme and gratuitous sex and violence may be contained in third party generated experience content. Users should read the experience content details before use. Use of third party generated experience content is at the users own risk and ZynnComm will not be held responsible as the supplier of the delivery platform.

CONTENT DEVELOPERS WARNING:

(a) The likeness of living individuals cannot be used to create dream immersion 'echoes' without their written permission.

(b) The likeness of deceased individuals cannot be used to create dream immersion 'echoes' without written permission from a family member or their legal representative.

(c) The likeness of copyrighted/trademarked characters, including deceased celebrated individuals, cannot be used to create dream immersion 'echoes' without written permission from the intellectual property owner or their legal representative.

(d) Trademark clearance must be sought by developers for the use of registered trademarks included in dream immersion

content. Written permission from the intellectual property
owner or their legal representative must be obtained.

Saxon left his office and entered the lab where Kris worked at a computer terminal. 'The actuary team have finished the draft for upfront guidelines and warnings for the platform.' He handed the document to Kris.

'No surprises?'

'Not really. We have to make sure users are aware.'

'I'm glad guideline three is in there after Merlin's little accident.'

'It was a cruel yet necessary experiment,' Saxon smiled.

'Have marketing put a retail price on the DI kit yet?'

'US, Yuan or Nukoin?'

'Nukoin,' Kris confirmed.

'Around 600 Nukoin was mentioned.'

'That's reasonable, about a fortnight's pay. Divide that by 365 days and it's only 1.64 Nukoin per experience. It's not cheap, but it's affordable.'

'It'll come down. We've got an advertising company onboard too, for product placements,' Saxon told him.

'I hope it's done subtly.'

'There are guidelines we have to follow. Now the word's out, the big advertisers are circling,' Saxon continued. 'And two major media corporations, an international gaming company and a European sporting network want to create dedicated networks for their content development and delivery.'

Kris smiled. 'Congratulations, Saxon, it's been a long journey.'

'I still feel apprehensive about bringing the launch forward,' Saxon confessed.

'I bet Walt and Alfred are pleased,' Kris said.

'They didn't say as much, but I think they'll be very pleased the income streams will finally start to flow.'

'We've got the meeting with all the codesters as soon as the gamers get back.'

'How long have they got?'

'About four minutes, if they make it through.'

'How many codesters do we have now?'

Kris was uncertain. 'About 47?' He tapped a nearby monitor and brought up a spreadsheet. 'Forty-nine.'

Their crafts flew past enormous asteroids four kilometres in width as they manoeuvred through the final stage of the asteroid belt course. Wendy was leading. Gravel sized debris to head sized rocks bombarded Merlin's windscreen and rebounded, his knuckles white as he wrestled the joystick. Red and yellow lights flashed in the distance on the largest asteroid in the sector, indicating the finish line.

'You're going down, Merlin!'

'Not if I can help it.' He lifted the cover guard protecting the hyperthruster but hesitated over the button. He activated autopilot first. Immediately, lightning-fast flight computers took control of hydraulic servo actuators utilising anticipatory guidance sensors to navigate the moving minefield. Now Merlin hit the hyperthruster.

'Thrust in three, two, one, ignition,' the craft reported. Merlin's vessel carved out a course to gain on Wendy, then overtook her.

'Slow down, Merlin, remember the retrograde orbiters are up ahead.'

At that moment, a significant boulder travelling against the orbit of most projectiles rose from Merlin's left and smashed into oncoming rocks, fragmenting debris in all directions. Merlin's craft almost made it past one immense splinter, but collided spraying sparks onto Wendy's vessel.

'Oooooouch!' Merlin howled, as his craft veered to the left and exploded on impact with the gnarly end of an asteroid.

The larger developer's lab on level three buzzed with anticipation as Saxon, Kris, Wendy, and Merlin exited the elevator.

'You did the same thing last time, Merlin. Why did you activate hyperthrusters again?' Wendy asked.

'I had to try.'

'Repeating the same thing over and over expecting a different result is—' Kris was cut off.

'I know, I know, the sign of a wicked pilot,' Merlin smirked.

'Can you make sure everyone's here, Merlin,' Wendy instructed.

Merlin skimmed through the sign-on device. 'Missing three. Good to go?' he asked.

Wendy looked at Saxon, who nodded.

'Listen up everyone. Hey, quiet please.' The ruckus continued. Merlin whistled, so loud it echoed throughout the lab, startling most.

'Thanks, Merlin,' Saxon cleared his throat to address the group. 'Welcome everyone. Thanks for attending this very important meeting. I'll get straight to it. We are accelerating the project with an anticipated soft launch in one month, the hard launch in early December, in time for Christmas.'

Instant murmurs erupted around the room.

'Do you think the platform will be ready in time, Saxon?' Someone asked from the middle of the crowd.

'I'm sure we'll have everything ready if we push ourselves. And that's—'

'Has it been fast tracked because of the media reports in the last 24 hours?' The same inquisitor made his way to the front. Sterling Lindquist was a unique looking individual, his facial embellishments made him so. Vibrant cosmetic tattoos highlighted his aqua dyed eyes and shock of red hair. 'Was that information meant to be released?'

Saxon gave Kris and Wendy a look of frustration. 'No, Sterling, it wasn't. There's an investigation underway at the moment. Having said that, it's important we use this to our advantage, which means ploughing through the projects we are currently working on to get the job done. Bonuses are on offer for those who put in an extra 12 hours per week, every week, for the next 15 weeks.'

Standing beside Sterling, Enzo Fontaine asked, 'How much?

'Five thousand Nukoin each,' Saxon responded.

'It should be more like 7,000 each,' Sterling added. 'Without us it doesn't happen.'

The assembly supported his logic.

Saxon smiled at Sterling before continuing. 'I'll tell you what I'll do. To put it simply, we need more experiences, more content. You are a unique group at this point in time, the master codesters who know how to write FH source code for Gatekeeper. You've all worked your arses off for the past year to get our content levels to this point, but we need more. Now that the precoding computers for routine elements are online, the process is quicker–'

Sterling piped up again. 'We're starting to lose codesters: Hendricks, Zhou and Oliveira have already been headhunted.'

Saxon turned to Kris. 'Is that true?'

'First I've heard of it, I'll have to check.'

Saxon turned back to the group. 'Okay, we'll be recruiting more codesters. I'll pay each of you a bonus of 8,000 Nukoin, but, and this is binding, only if all of you, every single one of you, agree to work the extra 12 hours per week over the next three months to get us to launch. If some of you don't wish to work the overtime, I'll pay those who have put in the extra hours a bonus of 6,000 Nukoin each.'

The room erupted in discussion. Huddles broke out as the codesters debated the options.

Kris, Wendy and Saxon also came together. 'That's a lucrative incentive, a lot of Nukoin,' Kris said.

'I'm prepared to go to 9,500 per person. Sterling's right, if we don't have them onside we don't launch.'

Sterling, Enzo, and a few others approached Saxon.

'Everyone has agreed to sign on,' Sterling said.

'Great to hear, thank you. I want you to be in charge of monitoring everyone's overtime for the next few months, Sterling.'

He looked surprised. 'I'm a developer, not a fucking payroll assistant!'

Saxon considered each of them individually, before resting his gaze back on Sterling. 'You initiated the negotiations, Sterling, and I'll stand by the deal if you agree to monitor everyone's time and if someone's not putting in, you kick their arse.'

Sterling searched the faces of his comrades before answering. 'Done,' he conceded.

Margo stood at the brushed stainless-steel kitchen island as Saxon entered their residence. 'I was just speaking to Robert–' she began.

'Robert?'

'Our next-door neighbour in Sydney.'

'Ahhh, you mean Bob!'

'His name is Robert. You're the only one who calls him Bob because you know he hates it.'

Saxon gave her a broad grin as he opened the refrigerator. 'What were you speaking to Bob about?' He took out a bottle of mineral water and poured a glass. 'Drink?'

She shook her head. 'I asked him to go over and check on Hugo.'

'How did he get in?'

'I gave him the code to the front gate.'

'And?'

'No sign of him, he didn't answer the door. I've tried everything. He's still not answering his PD,' she said, picking at her fingernails.

Saxon put his arms around Margo and held her. 'Do you want to fly to Sydney?'

'I'll...' At that moment Margo's PD buzzed and she pushed away from Saxon. 'It's a text from Hugo. *Keeping low profile because of media. H.*'

'Good, we know he's okay,' Saxon said with relief.

Margo was texting, not listening. 'I've asked him where he is. Funny, he's never signed off with a H before. I know it's from his PD, so why sign off?'

'Why didn't he tell us the other night he was going to ground so we didn't worry? Why does he want to get married? Why did he sign off with H? He's young...and thinks about one thing–himself.'

Margo's brow was furrowed. 'I think I'll fly to Sydney tomorrow.' She glanced back at her PD, willing a response from Hugo.

Chapter Four

The floating platform descended upwind of the massive erupting volcano Olympus Mons. Fumes ten kilometres high spewed hot ash and toxic gases into the Martian atmosphere.

'I really like this, Kris, you've created a spectacular event,' Saxon congratulated.

'It took me three months to create and almost three weeks to render it.'

Lena walked to the edge of the platform railing. 'I love that smell.'

'Looks great, Kris. When do we taste fire?' Merlin asked.

'Tasting fire! Yay!' Zen yelled.

'Try to appreciate the artistry of the experience, Merlin,' Saxon suggested.

'I do, I do, but I'm dying to find out the flavour of fire.'

'I think it'll be really hot and spicy, like chilli hot.' Zen offered.

The platform was bathed in an eerie orange hue as the distant midday Sun hid behind volcanic discharge. Kris steered the platform closer to the rim of the beast. Heat haze distorted the bubbling, oozing magma as they neared.

'It's getting hot,' Lena said.

'It's going to get hotter,' Kris told them. 'We're going to play with lava now.'

'Is this where we taste fire?' Merlin asked.

Kris manoeuvred the platform closer as fiery balls of magma shot into the air, almost hitting the ceramic platform. 'Move to the outside of the platform everyone and hold on to the railing.' Kris turned the platform quickly to the left and caught a huge dollop of molten lava in the middle of the platform. The blob burned red-hot as it quickly flattened to a pancake shape and began to crust.

'It's hot, like standing around a fire,' Zen commented. 'Who's got the marshmallows?'

Kris walked over to Merlin with a long, insulated straw. 'Have a taste,' he gestured to the burning mound with the straw. 'But be quick, or you'll singe your beard.'

Merlin took the straw and cautiously approached the congealing rock. He knelt, placed the straw into the dancing fire on the volcanic ejaculate, and sucked.

'Billboards and signage around the world are advertising The Event, social media is flooded with anticipation, and TV, radio and websites are saturated,' the TV interviewer announced. 'This morning, we welcome to the show the dream master himself, Dr Saxon Zynn, the man behind the Dream Immersion Platform and the frenzy gripping the world. Welcome, Dr Zynn.'

'Good morning.' Saxon was being broadcast from his office via a telepresencebot. Alfred, Wendy, and Kris stood behind the appliance, watching.

'Dr Zynn, where did the idea come from? When did the idea for dream immersion originate?'

'Well, Stark, the idea of dream manipulation isn't new, the idea has been around for the past couple of decades, but to author dreams from scratch using neural code is the idea I wanted to develop. I've never discussed this publicly before, but the idea came to me about 13 years ago while I was watering the garden.'

'So, the idea germinated in the garden so to speak,' Stark Green proposed, wearing a grin.

Saxon smiled awkwardly. 'Yes, I suppose it did. When I water the garden, I go into a contemplative state, it's very calming and I relax, and the creative juices start to flow. I thought about the possibility of mimicking our dream phases, to author new dreams. We are naturally capable of reproducing the same dreams more than once, such as in recurring dreams. So at first, it was a matter of understanding the stimulus that generated precisely timed spikes and firing rates of neural encoding and decoding and reproducing it.'

'And this started a decade long R&D process?'

'Correct.'

'How was dream immersion finally realised? Can you briefly explain how the technology came about, Dr Zynn?'

'I was researching and lecturing at the University of Oxford almost 12 years ago when Professor Eugene Mueller published his paper on Bioacoustic Cross Neural Sensory Stimulation. His paper changed my research approach. Since then, advances in neurochemistry, neurophysics, neuroinformatics, erm, neuromorphic and quantum computing has allowed us to synthesise very precise neural code, Synmem code, to mimic neurotransmission. Over the last few years we've been commercialising the platform utilising Gelchips.'

'Synmem code, that's the code you developed to deliver dream experiences?'

'Correct. Basically, Synmem code creates the chemical sequences needed for experiences, but the platform's backbone is our proprietary Norus network that harmonises all the elements to deliver dream immersion in real-time to millions of users worldwide simultaneously.'

'ZynnComm owns all the patents for the platform; from the software and hardware to the Norus network running the entire platform. ZynnComm is first to market with an extraordinary entertainment medium. Do you think competitors will be far behind in this innovative technology?' Stark posed.

'I'm certain we'll get imitators claiming they can deliver dream immersion, that's inevitable. When that will happen, I'm not sure. To achieve what ZynnComm will deliver shortly has taken a decade of hardcore research and development with substantial capital investment from the Tremaine Group. When you add the regulatory approval we've gained at every step of the process and all the intellectual property we've developed, I would like to think we'll be industry leaders for a few years at least.'

'From what I understand, dream immersion is relatively short, just 30 minutes or so.'

'Yes, dream immersion requires the brain to exert a massive amount of energy, so it's limited to 33 minutes as a safeguard. Our brain is the most complex organ in our bodies and it needs downtime. It requires us to shut down, to sleep, in order to function the next day, so we don't want to overexert it.'

'And what would happen if you pushed that timeframe out to say, 60 minutes?'

'Any longer could induce seizures, stroke, psychosis–'

'Oh? Okay...so you've found 33 minutes to be optimum?'

'Yes, we've spent years working through the science.'

'So, how much is an experience to purchase?'

'Users will buy credit in the currency of their choice and each experience will be about 15 US dollars, a little more if you don't want advertising.'

'None of us want ads.' Stark joked. 'This technology isn't bioware, it's not implanted in us is it?'

'No, no, it's external equipment, it's non-invasive, with a biosoftware component–'

'Biosoftware. Biosoftware makes people nervous, just walk us through what your biosoftware is.'

'Our biosoftware basically mimics our own biochemistry, it's a wafer called thalpherycine, that works with our Synmem code to deliver the dream immersion experience. The active ingredients dissolve soon after the experience. However I must reinforce, as a safety protocol users can only take part in dream immersion once in a 24-hour period. If they try to go a second time the hardware, the dream immersion dashboard and network, will deny access.'

'And that's the same for anyone under the age of 21, access is denied?'

'Absolutely, this entertainment experience is for adults only–'

'Why can't teenagers or children participate, Dr Zynn?'

'The brain isn't fully formed until we reach our 20's, so again, it's a safety protocol.'

'As is the intoxication rule.'

'Correct. Users will be denied access if they're intoxicated in any way.'

'I understand that dream immersion experiences are totally private, no one else can see which dream experience you've chosen?'

'Of course. As administrators, we can't see which experience users are in and no one else can unless they're invited to participate and have an access code. This was always a strict requirement for the platform, total privacy, the same as your organic dreams.'

'So wives won't know where their husbands are and vice versa?' Stark chuckled.

'Not unless they're sharing an experience.'

'Hmm, interesting. What happens if there's a power outage or the network lags under excessive use while in a dream experience?'

'There are backup generators at the Norus facility that kick in, so a blackout our end won't occur. If a power failure occurs anywhere between the facility and the end user, they simply wake up. As for network latency, quality of experience is paramount to us, so our network intelligence and connectivity management system, Jazper, guarantees lag or latency should never be an issue. Our Norus network can accommodate up to half a billion users simultaneously without any problems. Stage two of the network has begun, and that will accommodate a further billion users.'

'Are there any other health risks associated with dream immersion?'

'Our technology is based on our biological brain chemistry. There are some dream immersion experiences that will scare people, but those warnings are clearly explained before you enter, so it will be up to the user to decide if that experience is appropriate for them.'

'It goes beyond scaring people doesn't it? You mean they could die, don't you?'

'All users control their own risk level, their pain threshold, their safe word, and they can choose to remember or erase the experience. Dying in dream immersion is no different to dying in our organic nightly dreams. Some dreams are so realistic, so confronting we experience what we imagine is death. An automatic biological response releases a burst of adrenaline into our system so we wake up. Dream immersion is exactly the same. We've built in code to automatically release a surge of adrenaline to exit if death is experienced. We have to remember; this is an adult entertainment platform. All our testers are raving about it, they can't wait for the launch.'

'And the entertainment platform is for single and multiple users?'

'Absolutely. Individuals can have singular experiences or you can join a group experience, that's what our Dreamplexes will offer. Imagine arriving at a complex and taking part in a mass dream immersion experience with other Dreamplexes around the world, such as being in a crowd of a few thousand for a Rolling Stones or Beatles concert in the 1960s. The dream experience is enhanced by the human experience, being able to share the euphoria after an event by chatting about it and sharing on social media.

Although individual user preferences are customised for every player, experiences can be shared with friends in real time over consecutive experiences. Instead of roaming through a simulation wearing VR goggles, users will actually be on a battlefield on a distant planet smelling, feeling, experiencing everything, fighting aliens with their friends. Users will need to choose their experience carefully.'

'How do you think dream immersion will compete against entertainment juggernauts like exoskeletal extreme sports which has really captured public attention?'

'Yes, exoskeletal extreme sports are a spectacle, but they're professional sporting events, which are passive for spectators, very few can participate. Sport is actually one of the cornerstones of the platform. We have exoskeletal extreme sports in dream immersion that everyone can play, which are much more creative and exhilarating where players battle and compete against robots and aliens. To quote one of our catchphrases, "Everyone participates." While I'm with you, Stark, I'd like to announce the name of our retail entertainment division launching next month.'

'By all means, Dr Zynn,' Stark encouraged eagerly.

'Lucid. Lucid has a catalogue of entertainment experiences covering all genres: sport, gaming, drama, history, sci-fi, action, etcetera. All will be released in 26 languages. The other feature we offer is our intuitive international translator, allowing all users to interact in the language of their choice, so there are no language barriers.'

'That in itself is a unique selling point. As well as Lucid's catalogue of experiences, I understand any type of experience can be created using your Gatekeeper of Dreams engine?'

'Correct. Developers can be trained in Frequency Hypgenic or FH code for the Gatekeeper of Dreams authoring computer, or they can use our stock libraries and tools to create unique experiences, which will–'

'Spawn content production start-ups,' Stark finished.

'Exactly. When our dream immersion platform is released at Christmas, it will parallel, even surpass the experience of early cinema in the late 1800s, sparking human imagination and ingenuity to evolve beyond what we understand today, not only for those experiencing the medium but for those creating it.'

'So, you think the dream immersion platform will be an entertainment medium with longevity?'

'We anticipate the appetite for dream immersion will grow exponentially, Stark. But ultimately, the public will decide if the platform survives by investing their time, money and imagination.'

'We all know it'll be massive. Thank you, Dr Zynn.'

Saxon sat at his dining room table that evening reading the internal security report.

'*–there is convincing evidence that external technology penetrated our electronic surveillance system and accessed Raymond Bruce's personal device during the meeting exploiting it as a listening device. Raymond Bruce's device is a LineSat AS, model E3462, an older model with known vulnerability issues. Using GPS signatures, we traced the relay point from his PD to a vessel in Blanche Harbour, 25 kilometres south southeast of our facility. We intercepted and detained a yacht, named 'Blood Vessel II' sailing south in Spencer Gulf and turned two crew members over to federal authorities. A substantial amount of communications equipment was found aboard the vessel.*

Blood Vessel II relayed the transmission to 23a Valley Rd., Singapore. The house is a rental property owned by Alphebus Property Holdings Pte Ltd, a subsidiary of parent corporation, Goodman-Black Inc. registered in Cheyanne, Wyoming, USA. Investigations have revealed the property is not currently rented and has been vacant for two months.

There is no evidence that Raymond Bruce was directly involved, however we will have Mr Bruce under 24-hour surveillance for the next six-months–'

Saxon's device buzzed, prompting him to put the document aside. It was Margo.

'He's gone to Hawaii!' Margo gushed before her projection was out of his device.

'That's definite?'

'I've just spoken to Heather, Christine's mother. She's beside herself. And guess why they really want to get married?'

'Be–'

'She's pregnant! Christine's pregnant!'

'Shit,' Saxon said under his breath. 'Heather told you that?'

Margo began to weep. 'Yes. Christine told her last week, before they announced the wedding plans.' She wiped her eyes. 'FUCK! You never know until your child has grown up if you did a good job, it's a fucking lucky dip, and we–'

'Margo, sweetie, listen to me. Being hard on yourself isn't productive.' Saxon placed his device on the table.

'He lied to us! He said he was in hiding. He's only known this girl for six months! Just another one of his damn projects he dabbles in for a while before he moves on to the next one. You know, this is Mexico all over again, he just up and disappears.'

'It sounds like Christine is more than a project. He probably thinks he's doing the honourable thing. Let's think this through.'

'I've tried his friends over the last couple of days, and checked with the uni, that's how I got Heather's number. Then she tells me she got a text from Christine yesterday saying they were going to Hawaii. Heather's flying to Hawaii tomorrow, I'm going with her.'

'Okay, that sounds like a plan. Have they been married? Does she know if they've been married?'

'No,' she replied despondently.

'No they haven't or no she doesn't know?'

'She doesn't know.'

'Where are they staying?'

'Not with her family. Heather's sister is checking for us.'

A thought-filled pause penetrated the conversation.

'I wish he could've just told us about the situation from the beginning,' Saxon confessed.

'They probably thought they couldn't wait any longer, she's already a month gone Heather said.'

'Have you called the Australian Consulate-General? Get them to track him down.'

'I tried earlier, but Hawaii's 21 hours behind Sydney, they were closed. I'll call in the morning.' The silence grew into seconds. 'I saw your interview earlier, you did really well,' Margo finally said.

'You know I hate doing media, thanks for the heads up,' he said sarcastically.

'I know, but Dad asked me to organise something quickly to capitalise on the momentum. You came across so well. I didn't know Lucid was going to be mentioned today?'

'I figured if I'm promoting, I might as well get the name of our entertainment division out there from the start.' Saxon glanced at the report on the table. 'I was just re-reading the investigation report into the leak? Have you read it? Ray Bruce's PD was hacked.'

'I skimmed through it. I still think the leak will be positive.'

'You're biased—seems I'm in bed with a sympathiser.'

'It's my job, darling,' she paused. 'Pregnant! Stupid bloody kids.'

'It's lucky they've both got wealthy parents,' Saxon baited.

'No way. He's got his trust; he can access that in a year. He needs to take responsibility.'

Saxon yawned. 'I'm off to bed. I'll call you in the morning. Love you, sweetie.'

'Love you, darling, good night.'

As day broke in south-eastern France, May 1942, three men each carrying a Sten submachine gun, scampered across a ploughed field towards a timber framed house. They crept around the side of the house to the back door.

Kris cautiously opened the door, surprising a middle-aged woman and a teenage girl cooking in the small kitchen. Kris put his index finger to his mouth in a gesture of silence.

The woman and girl stood motionless, then looked at each other then back at Kris.

A vehicle could be heard as it approached the house along the only dirt road.

'Open the floor hatch,' the woman instructed the girl before she waved Kris and the other men in. 'One of you in there,' she pointed to the floor. The second man jumped into the opening and the young girl closed the hatch and placed a rug over it. The woman walked over to the wall, pushed on it and it popped open. 'One in here.' Kris got into the wall cavity. 'Here,' the woman pulled a rope hanging from the ceiling and a panel and ladder dropped down. The last man scurried up the ladder and the girl pushed the ladder back up and hid the rope.

A military vehicle pulled up in front of the house and three Italian soldiers and an officer got out. Two soldiers immediately stood guard either end of the vehicle. The officer waited as his attendente opened the front door of the house, then stepped aside. The officer walked straight through to the kitchen while his man remained at the front door.

Kris watched the teenage girl through a crack in the wall as she acknowledged the officer. She then pointed to the floor, wall, and ceiling. His heart began to race. He remembered the orders he and the other two men were given; *stop the information being carried by the officer in the vehicle from reaching HQ in the nearby town before nightfall or hundreds of undercover resistance fighters will be exposed.* Kris had to make a moral decision, kill everyone in the room or just the officer.

'Do you have food for my men?' the officer asked the woman.

'Of course, bread and cheese.'

'Thank you.' The officer looked around the room before focusing on the young girl. 'Have you seen any strangers in the area?'

'No, sir.'

'I'll get my men, they are very hungry,' the officer said, then left the room.

Kris quietly pushed his way out of the wall cavity. The woman was about to yell as Kris rested the gun muzzle against her cheek. He threw a threatening look at the girl. 'Carven, get out,' Kris whispered to the man under the floor. 'Come down, Girard,' he said to the man in the ceiling.

Three soldiers entered the kitchen as both men were exiting their hiding holes. Girard managed to kill one of the soldiers as he jumped from the ladder. Carven was shot in the head before he could get out of the floor space, and Kris shot a second soldier dead.

The woman picked up a pistol from the cupboard and handed it to the girl as Girard shot the third soldier. The girl shot Girard point blank in the chest while the woman grabbed another pistol.

Kris made a split-second decision to kill the females or be killed, as he heard the vehicle engine start outside. He sprayed the kitchen with a volley of rounds killing the girl. Kris was hit in the arm from the woman's weapon as she collapsed, wounded. She lifted her arm to squeeze off another shot, as Kris peppered her with bullets. He ran out the front of the house to see the vehicle driving off. He fired for a few seconds, but the vehicle was out of range. Spying a motorcycle near a shed, he jumped on and tried to start it.

From behind him, a farmer snuck out from the shed and fired a single shot into the back of Kris' head.

Saxon joined Merlin and Kris as they watched a news report on a monitor in the lab.

'Look at this,' Kris said to Saxon.

'You think this new dream immersion technology will impact your religion?' The interviewer asked.

'It's blasphemy! Dream immersion technology is an abomination, it's simply not a natural process.' The onscreen graphic read, *Jeremy Abernathy – Fundamental Purists Founder/Leader.* 'I deliver the word of our God to our followers in their dreams. My sermons are recorded, my disciples listen to them as they go to sleep and God speaks to them in their dreams offering guidance and direction.'

'How many followers do you have?'

'Millions,' Abernathy boasted.

The segment finished as a TV anchor-woman appeared on screen.

'That was Jeremy Abernathy, the founder and leader of the Fundamental Purists. From our investigations, there are just over 650,000 supporters of his movement worldwide. They are emerging as one of the most vocal groups opposing ZynnComm's dream immersion technology.'

An advertisement for Golden Ox Neomeat popped onto the screen. Merlin switched it off. 'Golden Ox is the best.'

'I've never been a fan of shmeat,' Kris said.

'Not as expensive as the real thing and it smells and tastes just like meat.'

'Not like fire?' Kris goaded with a grin.

Merlin looked at Kris with disdain. 'It doesn't taste like your damn awful fire. I can still taste that horrible, shitty taste in my mouth you bastard.'

Saxon and Kris laughed at Merlin.

'I've told you about Amanda Voss,' Saxon said.

'Oxford colleague?' Kris asked.

Saxon nodded. 'After she left Oxford in 2041 she moved to the US and married Abernathy.'

'That's one weird religion,' Merlin said. 'A cousin of mine was briefly involved with them. She tried to get me to read his book, The Great...um–'

'Occurrence,' Saxon finished. 'He registered his religion four years after he self-published the book in 2035. It has made him a rich man.'

'My cousin used to work at one of their organic chicken meat outlets,' Merlin said. 'She got paid minimum wage, and they turned over a shitload of chickens she said. They have to wear 100 percent pure cotton clothing, eat no processed foods, no preservatives and additives, wash in fresh or ocean water, oh, and have lots of sex.'

Kris considered Merlin for a moment with a sly grin. 'And you didn't join?'

'I actually considered it for like, ten minutes, but no, no, it's not for me.'

'Did you test Kurt's game?' Saxon asked Kris.

'I really got into it, it was challenging because of the moral dilemma,' Kris explained.

'Yeah, me too. Did you kill the officer?'

'He failed the mission, the officer with the information got through,' Merlin taunted.

'I'll do things differently next time,' Kris admitted.

'The scenario changes every time you play,' Saxon told him. 'In one of mine the soldiers threaten to torture the older woman, in another, the girl–'

'That's so cool!' Merlin said. 'Not the torture, the arbitrary game change feature. I knew they were working on it. I'll try it tonight.'

'It's still early days, but random variations on the theme are possible across three levels.'

'I remember my father showing me Second World War photos in 2024, that my great -great grandfather took in New Guinea,' Kris contemplated aloud. 'I must have been about 17 I suppose. US Merchant Marines were playing soccer with the heads of executed Japanese prisoners. I'll always remember that,' Kris paused, refocusing on Saxon. 'Did you stop the officer getting through?'

'Sure did,' Saxon replied with confidence as his PD could be heard buzzing in his office, 'on my fourth go. I've got to get that.'

'Can't find either of them,' Margo reported calling from Hawaii. 'I'm at the Australian Embassy now, they're cross-referencing flight records with passport and hotel records for the last few days. We've located three of his mates, they're in Kahului on Maui. Last time they saw Hugo and Christine was in Sydney two days ago.' Someone called to Margo in the background. 'Sorry, I have to go, darling, I'll call you as soon as I have news.' She disconnected.

A new email alert appeared on Saxon's device, a second email from Scarlett Drummond, the woman he had worked with at Oxford University years ago.

'Heard from Hugo?' Scarlett.

Saxon was confused. He hadn't seen or heard from Scarlett in years, and now two emails in a week. Saxon spoke her name into the search engine on his device. The first search result added to his confusion.

'Dr Scarlett Drummond's body found in wreckage of a light plane crash, June 19th, 2047'.

Saxon stared at his device perplexed, that was two months ago.

Chapter Five

Wendy strapped herself into the single seat. The restrictive cockpit was embedded in the breast of an oversized African glossy-starling. She adjusted her snug fitting helmet and thought, *'take off.'* Instantly, the starling leapt from the platform and began to flap its wings madly to gain altitude. The pair flew up over a purple forest towards the setting sun. Wendy thought, *'dive'*, and the bird tucked in its wings and obeyed. Wendy loved the sensation of falling at speed. As they hurtled towards the ground Wendy thought, *'level out, bank right, join the flock'*.

At sunset, through warm hazy air, a black swarm swooped, soared and absorbed her bird into the murmuration of starlings. The aerial ballet that was awe-inspiring to watch, was even more fascinating to be part of, sharing in the fluid magic. Wendy melted into the spontaneously choreographed cast of thousands whirling, rippling, waving, rolling, separating, merging. The coordination and communication within the collective creature was instantaneous. The contorted iridescent ribbon twisted into a thin shadowy line then surged to explode into a satin balloon reflecting the sunlight, before swirling around into a tornado of congested wings. The synchronised dance lasted many minutes until Wendy broke away elated, and the flock settled in the trees, preparing for the next act.

Merlin shoved his device in Wendy's face while she was still lying on the sleep pod.

'Check this out, me with Uncle Walt on the Tremaine Group news feed.'

'Wonderful. Where's Kris?'

'Down with the codesters. More have been headhunted,' he said, putting his device away. 'How was it?'

'Fucking fantastic. There's a couple of tweaks to be made, but very minor.' Wendy removed her DI dashboard and got off the sleep pod. 'Anything from Saxon?'

'Nope.'

'Did he say anything to you about Hugo before he left?' she asked.

'As if.'

'What does that mean?'

'I don't know Hugo. I think I've met him once in the five years I've been here.'

'I just thought he might have said something.'

'Nope.'

Wendy stretched. 'I need a boost. You hungry?'

'Extremely.'

Saxon stood with his eyes closed listening to music, waiting for Margo. He felt the light rain on his eyelids. The tranquil moment was disturbed by the buzz of his PD. Reluctantly, he opened his eyes and touched the voice call icon.

'I'm just coming into the airport now,' Margo said.

'I'm out front.' Saxon watched as Margo's vehicle approached in the distance and pulled up at the curb. Saxon greeted her with a wet, hungry kiss. 'I've missed you.'

'Me too. Change of plan, the detectives are meeting us at home,' Margo told him. The rain got heavier as she closed the cabin door and touched *Home* on the navigation dash.

'Why?'

'They want to check his room. They said because he hasn't used his passport, there might be some clues to where he is.'

'Sounds a bit cloak and dagger,' Saxon suggested. 'He'll turn up in a few days and make us look like fools again.'

'He'd better. What have you been listening to?'

'Bit of old stuff, Mr Cohen. Trying to get my mind off things.' His device buzzed again.

Alfred's head projected from Saxon's device. 'Good morning, Saxon, Margo.'

'Morning, Alfred. Any news?'

'Chen's team has gathered some information. Oxford University confirmed Scarlett Drummond's email had in fact been hacked and her address has now been deleted from their system. The emails you received both originated in Scotsdale, Missouri, USA. The population is only 402. Chen said a VPN concealed the actual location of the sender and will never be found. Scarlett Drummond died in a plane crash along with her husband and two children flying out of Pitt Meadows Airport, just east of Vancouver. They were on vacation, heading to Kamloops in British Columbia. Her husband was a registered pilot and he had hired the aircraft. The wreckage was found in a remote area of the Golden Ears Provincial Park, a week after it was reported missing. The Transportation Safety Board of Canada has opened an investigation into the crash, but it will take months before the official report is released. However, local speculation says the crash was due to poor weather conditions.'

'So, what's the connection to Hugo?' Saxon questioned.

'We are not sure at this stage.'

'We're meeting with detectives shortly. Send me that information and I'll pass it on.'

'Of course. Chen has also traced the meeting leak back to Northrup Merged Media. One of their online outlets broke the story. I am meeting with legal tomorrow to see if we have cause to pursue them...one moment please.' Alfred was speaking to someone off camera. 'You need to see this; I have sent you the link. I will contact Walt.' Alfred disconnected.

Saxon tapped on the video link.

The recording showed two hooded figures seated in chairs. Someone off screen removed the hoods to reveal Hugo and Christine.

Margo gasped as she grabbed Saxon's arm. 'No...no, no, no, nooo,' Margo howled.

Christine sobbed as she was handed a tablet device.

'Hold it up to the camera,' a female voice off screen ordered.

Christine extended her shaky arms, so the tablet was close to the camera.

'Keep it still bitch!'

It showed a live webcam feed of Shibuya Crossing in Tokyo with today's date and time. It was just ten minutes old. Someone pulled the tablet from her hands.

'Read the message,' a male voice demanded of Hugo.

In an unsteady voice Hugo began to read the message that was being held off screen. 'If you want us back alive...' he paused.

'Read the fucking message!' A captor barked.

'You must abandon the technology. Do not release the dream immersion platform to the public. You have 48 hours to publicly comply. I'm so sor–' The video stopped.

'Oh, Hugo, Hugo. Fuck, Saxon! What can we do?' Margo melted, distraught. 'How do we get him back?'

Saxon called Walt at once. 'Have you seen the video?'

'I don't know what to say,' Walt apologised.

'Get him back, Walt,' Saxon stressed. 'You know people who can get him back.'

'Of course.' Walt disconnected.

Rain pelted the vehicle windscreen as Saxon put his arms around his shaking, wailing wife. His thoughts ran helter skelter. He had no words to console her–there were no words. The helplessness, the fear, the turmoil welled up and spilled down his cheeks.

An hour later, Saxon and Margo were in the living room of their Sydney harbourside home as the rain continued to fall. The stylish room was littered with photos of Hugo at various stages of his life. Margo monitored comments on social media about the ransom video that had exploded and gone viral, while Saxon inspected their garden from afar.

'Early spring, kangaroo paw has already started to flower,' he commented.

Margo was absorbed, she didn't respond.

In the dining room, two detectives had arranged a make-shift office on their table.

'Look at this, Dave,' Detective Temple said.

Detective Kane ended his voice call and wandered over to the computer. 'The audio forensic team are analysing the voices and atmosphere in the recording. What is it?'

'I've broken the footage down frame by frame and enhanced it. Look at this.' He pointed to a reflection in the tablet device that Christine held up. 'See that?'

Detective Kane squinted to make it out. 'Not really, what do you think it is?'

'It's a small logo on a t-shirt. It's the reverse of this.' He opened another window on the computer showing a woman wearing a t-shirt with a logo. 'FP, see?' He moved both windows side by side.

'Fuck me. It's them. Minimise the t-shirt image.' Detective Kane said, before he strode into the living room. 'Could you both take a look at this please.'

'What is it?' Margo asked anxiously, following Saxon into the dining room.

Saxon and Margo both stared quizzically at the freeze frame on the computer.

'What is it?' Saxon asked.

'Do you recognise it?' Detective Kane questioned.

Saxon shook his head.

'What is it?' Margo repeated.

'It's a reflection on the tablet that Christine held up,' Detective Temple explained.

'Open the other window Mo,' Detective Kane directed.

He opened the other window showing the t-shirt beside the freeze frame.

'FP?' Margo said.

'Fundamental Purists,' Saxon said quietly.

'This ties in with the emails you received,' Detective Kane said.

'That bitch Amanda Voss is involved in this,' Margo accused.

'Possibly. Amanda Voss is married to Jeremy Abernathy and he has publicly opposed your technology, so there is a connection,' Detective Kane said.

'It's a pity Scarlett Drummond's email has been deleted, we could have used it to contact them,' Saxon pondered aloud.

'Were you able to trace the text I received from Hugo last week? Was there a GPS location?' Margo asked.

'The message originated in Sydney, but the GPS was disabled. The device is off network now.' Detective Temple informed her. 'Same with Christine's device used to contact Mrs Knox, saying they were going to Hawaii.'

'Can't you trace the chipset in their PD's?' Saxon asked.

'They have to be on,' Detective Temple explained. 'Anyway, we need a court order since the privacy laws changed.'

'Even in cases of kidnapping?' Margo pushed.

'It'll take a couple of days to get one. We have other avenues we can pursue. What I'm about to tell you isn't public knowledge,' Detective Kane began. 'The Fundamental Purists have been on our radar here in Sydney for the past few months. Outspoken ex-members of the religion have been abducted, just for a few days, never harmed but threatened, then released. It's a scare tactic that shuts them up. Much of the evidence has been hearsay because ex-members won't talk or press charges. This is different. If it's the same group, they've changed their MO on this one. Up until now they haven't asked for anything. They've evolved from abductions to kidnapping. This recording is a first from the group and it's a game changer. This evidence links FP directly to the kidnapping.'

'But does it go all the way to Abernathy?' Saxon questioned.

Detective Kane looked at his partner before answering. 'It's a possibility. Our US colleagues have been investigating Abernathy for the past year, regarding a similar pattern of abductions of vocal ex-members. But again, it's difficult to prove if no one is willing to talk.'

Saxon looked at his watch. 'So how do we get them back with just under 47 hours left before we have to release a statement?'

'This is a time sensitive operation, but you never give kidnappers what they want, or make concessions–'

'What?' Margo exploded. 'Of course we give them what they want, they could kill our son!'

Detective Kane held his palms up in a calming gesture to Margo. 'I completely understand your response, it's a parent's response, that unbreakable bond driving you to move heaven and earth to gain their release. I'd expect the same if it were my kids, you don't want to gamble with their lives. It's a gut-wrenching dilemma whether to give in to abductors, to jeopardise innocent loved ones,' he paused. 'But, if you give into their demands it increases the risk of further abductions, it motivates groups like this to continue to take other innocent people. Cancelling the release and shutting down your platform won't resolve this. We negotiate.'

'I don't give a fuck if it motivates them to do this again! I want Hugo back.' Margo shared her anguished expression with Saxon. Her tone now solemn. 'What are the chances of getting them back alive, detective?'

'Statistically, about 58 percent. But you have a better chance than most, because of your business connections, you have more options. Consider engaging a private risk management company. As police, we can't endorse that option, but we can't stop you either. Chances of a safe return are higher if you have a risk management team working with you.'

'We have to get our son back at any cost,' Margo declared. 'If we have to shut down the platform we do it.'

'Of course,' Saxon agreed. 'Walt is handling risk management, but he won't shut down the project without an almighty jolt from you.'

'You're right,' Margo concurred. 'I'll talk to him. In the meantime, the fucking media drones are already camped outside our front gate. I'll ask Selma to handle the press on this, I can't do it.'

Merlin and Zen stood side by side, a few metres apart, on the precipice looking down. Both wore full face helmets decorated to resemble evil skulls. The salmon coloured sky appeared painted with wispy blue clouds. Visibility was perfect. Yet when they stared over the cliff, very little could be distinguished at the bottom many kilometres below.

'Are you ready?' Merlin asked.

'I think so,' came her response through his helmet audio. 'This is crazy.'

'It is. I like crazy–wakes up the brain cells,' Merlin admitted.

'The risk factor is low, right?' Zen confirmed. 'You're sure we don't need a parachute or a wingsuit?'

'Positive. Try to stay level, belly to the ground and spread eagle. Ready?'

'Let's go. Three, two, one, gooo!'

Zen simply fell forward off the cliff, while Merlin leapt off in a majestic swan dive. Gravity promptly pulled them towards the ground with extreme prejudice.

'Yeeeehaaaa!' Zen yelled.

'Too loud Zen,' Merlin grumbled. The sensation of free falling thrilled Merlin, it was his ultimate exhilarating experience. A patchwork of country fields stretched on for kilometres below as he accelerated faster and faster reaching terminal velocity at almost 200 kilometres an hour. Merlin felt like he was floating, not falling, soaring not plummeting. The timecode overlay on his visor hit 60 seconds. 'Seven minutes before we hit.'

'I love this feeling.'

'Transcendent.' Merlin was suspended in the wonder of falling through sky, never afraid during the descent. Just falling. It was the freest place he had ever been. The real world that restricted him was gone. His mind wandered off into far flung reflections.

Minutes later a beep in his ear focused his thoughts. 'Prepare for impact,' Merlin warned.

'Will it hurt?'

'Nah, not a bit.' At that moment they both came into contact with the safety web and instantly stuck. The sticky mesh distorted under the strain of catching them, interrupting gravity. Once the net reached full expansion, the mesh recoiled up, then back down, up, down, until it came to rest.

'This is a cool fucking ride, Merlin.'

Merlin thought, *'deactivate web'* . The pair stood up. 'It is. We just fell 24 kilometres in eight minutes. We have time for two more jumps and the next one...is in the dark through fireworks.'

'Awesome!' Zen squealed.

They walked to the edge of the net and dove into a tube slide that delivered them to the ground.

'In here,' Merlin directed. They entered an elevator and sat in two luxurious chairs cradling their calves and forearms in padded rests. Merlin pressed the only button on the wall, *'Up.'* The doors closed, and they accelerated at speed back to the top.

That afternoon, Saxon was exercising on the elliptical cross trainer in his gym when Walt called.

'We've arranged to meet with US authorities in New York in a few hours,' Walt said. 'We'll be pushing for action against Abernathy.'

'You've spoken to Detective Kane?' Saxon got off the machine, panting.

'Yes, and Margo. She told me Selma's taking the lead on PR. She'll release a statement tomorrow.' An awkward silence lingered. 'How are you holding up? You're breathing hard.'

'Exercising, trying to keep my mind off it,' he caught his breath. 'But I can't. I'm...I'm sort of numb, still trying to process all the what if's,' Saxon explained as he sat.

'I know what you mean, I've been doing the same,' Walt admitted. 'Margo's putting on a brave face; how is she really?'

'She was a mess at first, but you know Margo, she's a strong, pragmatic woman. She's coping.' He wiped the sweat from his face with his towel.

'She has her mother's stoicism.'

'Get them back, Walt. I don't know how we'd cope if–'

'We'll get them back. I've got a team from Firerock on it.'

'Covert hostage recovery, right?'

'Yep, best in the business and we own them. They'll find them, and once they're safe we'll continue with the platform roll out.'

'And what if this happens again? I don't want to keep looking over my shoulder, Walt."

'We've spent billions of dollars on this project, no release is not an option. If a few extremists have to be removed along the way, so be it. If you and the family require around the clock security, we do it. Don't think for one second the platform won't be released Saxon, it will, and it'll be a massive success.'

Saxon thought about his words for a moment. 'I don't think you understand the strength of our resolve on this, Walt,' Saxon spelt it out. 'We are talking about Hugo, your grandson, our flesh and blood. If Margo and I have to choose between Hugo or the platform, it will be Hugo.'

'We'll get them back Saxon,' Walt repeated. 'I have to go. We'll talk later.' Walt disconnected.

Saxon sat motionless for a long time listening to his breathing, his mind swimming. He then realised he was staring at a photo hanging on the wall. He was compelled to get up and walk over to it. The photo was of Hugo when he was five. It was taken on his first day at school, the same day Saxon's sister, Lena, died. His gaze panned across to Hugo's gravity inversion table in one corner of the gym. *Hugo loves that machine*, he thought. Saxon found himself still running through the what if's. He rationalised three possible outcomes: Hugo is released quickly, Hugo is kept for a period of time but ultimately released, or Hugo is killed. Saxon stood and stared at the photo for some time, evaluating the probabilities for each, contemplating the consequences that could flow from those scenarios.

Kris and Wendy were working in the lab when Merlin arrived in the elevator studying his PD. 'Check this out,' he said as he projected his screen onto the lab wall. They both wandered over to watch.

'Breaking News' graphics scrolled along the bottom of the screen before footage of men in suits appeared bundling another man into the back seat of a vehicle.

The voiceover said, 'In breaking news, Jeremy Abernathy, the founder and leader of the Fundamental Purists movement, has been detained for questioning by the FBI in Mississippi. The FBI have not yet commented on the reason for Mr Abernathy's detention at this stage.' Merlin shut it off.

'Coincidence?' Kris suggested. 'Methinks not.'

'They have motive,' Wendy said as she returned to her work. 'Not arrested, just questioning the report said.'

'Could be a bargaining chip for Hugo and Christine's release,' Kris offered. 'If he's involved.'

'True,' Merlin said.

'Saxon wouldn't have that much clout would he?' Wendy queried.

'Definitely Walt's doing,' Kris said.

'Of course,' Wendy agreed. 'They must have found a connection to Abernathy.'

'I wouldn't want to be in Saxon's shoes for all the Nukoin on Earth,' Kris said. 'Margo and Saxon are in a precarious position, there's not much wiggle room.'

'They may be able to haggle now,' Merlin said quietly.

'I don't want to think about it,' Wendy said as her PD buzzed, simultaneously with Kris' and Merlin's. They all read the same text message.

'*To all staff, Zynn Communications and the Tremaine Group will not be forced into cancelling the release of our Dream Immersion Platform. The release will go ahead as planned. A media release will be issued tomorrow. Thank you. Selma Thurston, Operations Manager, ZynnComm Public Relations.*'

'Holy shit,' Merlin said.

'Game on. Walt is known for playing hard,' Kris said.

'Let's hope it works,' Wendy offered. 'How's the codester recruiting going?' She shifted the conversation.

'The agency sent me a list of five applicants they cleared this morning,' Kris answered. 'Interviewing tomorrow for immediate start.'

'Bennet and Laurent gave their notice today,' Merlin said. 'Headhunted by Electronic Artists, a dream phaze startup.'

'Fuck! At this rate we'll be out of codesters before we launch,' Kris said, 'I need to speak to Alfred about the FH codester training program. We need to cast our net wider.'

'What do you mean by dream phaze startup?' Wendy questioned Merlin.

'Dream phaze is an expression being used in forums and chat rooms. It's being used to distinguish engineered dreams from our natural dreams. Phaze is spelt P-H-A-Z-E. You don't monitor the forums that have popped up since we went public?'

'Dream phaze,' Wendy repeated. 'Erm, no, no I don't have time. Don't need to, you do it.' She smiled.

Saxon sat in the living room watching a documentary on ecoterrorism.

'In the northern winter of 2031, the Coal Conflicts began,' the voice over said. 'Ecoterrorists targeted the remaining coal-fired power plants in the U.S from Michigan to Texas. The Coal Conflicts prompted the first use of semi-autonomous robotic troops developed in the United States to be deployed on home soil in the fight against home grown terrorism.' Footage showed elongated six-legged robots traversing rugged terrain towards a terrorist stronghold, firing dual mounted machine guns. Drone bombers could be seen in the background firing missiles in the same direction then peeling off. 'The Red Eagle Militia, or REM as they were known, led by Lena Zynn and Michael Strathmore, were secretly funded by–'

Saxon's PD buzzed him back into the room and present day. He muted the monitor as Walt's head projected from his device.

'Abernathy's detention will buy us time while the Firerock team get set-up for an extraction,' Walt said.

'Have they found him?' Saxon blurted.

'They will, it's just a matter of time. They have access to tech that most don't. They've never failed to find a package.'

'Shit, Walt, package? Really?'

'Sorry,' he apologised.

'Have they got anything on Abernathy? Can they charge him?'

'Nothing linking him directly with the kidnapping at this stage, but it's early days,' Walt explained. 'They can hold him for 14 days without charge while they do a forensic audit of his business if they want.'

'We saw the text from Selma, I hope this strategy doesn't backfire.' His attention was side-tracked by an ad on his muted monitor for The Event, with the catchphrase, '*Everyone has a second life in dream immersion*.'

'We're lucky we had the Abernathy card to play, I don't know what we would've done without it.'

'Do you think Abernathy would have actually ordered the kidnapping?' Saxon asked.

'It doesn't matter, FP are directly involved, Abernathy indirectly at this stage. I wouldn't put it past Abernathy...' Walt hesitated. 'But the–'

'But what?'

Walt remained silent for a moment. 'The main reason for the call was...I found out today I have to go in for another liver transplant.'

'Fuck Walt! Didn't you get a new liver a couple of years ago?'

'I did, almost to the day. Lucky I've got a few in storage ready to go–'

'Have you told Margo?'

'Not yet, she's got enough stress. That's where you come in my boy.'

'Nope.' Saxon said flat-out. 'This is your responsibility, Walt. You do the damage; you do the explaining.'

'Saxon, please?' Walt implored.

'I'll tell you what. You give up drinking 25-year-old scotch whisky and I'll be your messenger boy.'

'That defeats the purpose of getting a new liver. Besides, this one was a fucking dud, the last liver lasted six years.'

'This'll be your fourth liver transplant–'

'Fifth.

'Shit!'

'Look, Saxon, if there's one thing I'm going to spend my truckloads of money on it is spare parts. If they can print 'em, I'll use 'em.'

'You can't replace your brain, Walt, you can't do without that.'

'True, but I get new blood each year, a new heart every three years, if I need it or not–'

'How old are you, Walt, 88?'

'Eighty-nine.'

'It's time you grew up. That's the deal, you stop drinking and I'll tell Margo. Otherwise, you're on your own.'

'Fine, I'll tell her myself.'

At that moment Margo walked into the room.

'Good, here she is now.'

Walt immediately disconnected.

'Was that, Dad?'

'Yep. He had to go. He'll call you tomorrow.'

'I need a cuddle,' Margo said snuggling into Saxon. 'What are you watching?'

'Doco on ecoterrorism.'

'Have they mentioned Lena?'

'There was a reference to her earlier, but then Walt called.'

'How long has it been now?'

'Fifteen years.'

Margo looked up at him confused, doing the math. '2032. Yeah, it is. That's gone so quickly. Hugo was starting school.'

'Yep. But she's still with us.'

'She is.'

'Did you want to watch something?'

'No, it's almost midnight.' She settled back into him. 'Let's turn it off and just sit. It's been a long day.'

Saxon switched off the wall screen with a wave of his hand, then hugged his wife.

Chapter Six

Made with wattle and daub walls, the thatched roof longhouse was smoke-filled and smelled of pig shit. Children made faeces balls and threw them at each other as women served mead to groups of huddled men. The huge fire in the centre blazed, keeping everyone warm.

Kris grabbed a horn filled with mead from a table and wandered over to a group of gruesomely disfigured men. He watched in astonishment as a grimy older man casually filed the front teeth of an unflinching younger man with a crude metal instrument. His gums and lips dripped with blood. When the old man paused, the bloodied man took several gulps of mead, washing away the blood, exposing a series of horizontal lines filed into his teeth, before repositioning his grisly mouth for further punishment.

'Last one,' the old man announced. 'Hold still.'

'Me next,' a ginger bearded man said. His head was shaven on both sides leaving a Mohawk-style strip down the centre. His left ear had a bite mark out of it; the other was completely gone.

'I am next!' An extremely hairy, darker man contested. His nose sat squashed on his face, with a ragged scar running from the left corner of his mouth to the corner of his left eye. 'Agnar, I am next.'

'I don't care who is next, you work it out,' old man Agnar said.

With that, the ginger bearded man leapt to his feet and smashed the darker man squarely in the face with his sizable fist, driving him backwards. Agnar continued to file as the huddle broke up to watch the fight.

The dark man got to his feet. 'Thane, you surprised me with your smack.'

'I'm next, Arvid. I've been waiting longer,' Thane said.

Kris stepped sideways, giving the two Norsemen a wide berth as they postured for position.

Arvid lunged at Thane, grabbing his plaited beard, and cracking his head on the chunky timber tabletop. A bloody-faced Thane snatched a long dagger from the table, spun around and thrust it up into Arvid's soft fleshy under jaw, jamming it in as far as it would go, until the blade protruded from the top of his head.

A loud cheer erupted from the small, appreciative crowd.

'I told you. I was next,' Thane said, pulling the weapon from Arvid's head.

'Valhal...' Arvid gurgled as he collapsed.

Merlin walked quietly over to Enzo Fontaine who was hunched over a bench in the main developers' lab snoozing. Merlin took out his PD and tapped the screen before he held it to Enzo's ear. A blood curdling scream exploded from the device.

Enzo jumped up, startled, and fell off his stool.

Merlin cracked up laughing. 'You're about as useful as a resuscitation unit in an aged care home.'

Enzo sat on the floor disorientated for a moment. 'Fuck you,' he finally said. He picked himself up. 'It's late and I've been here since six this morning.'

'So have I!'

'I haven't been well the last couple of days,' Enzo added. 'What are you doing here anyway?' Enzo checked his braided orange ponytail before he sat back on his stool.

'I'm under so much pressure, I'm almost a diamond,' Merlin whinged.

'You, a diamond? Fuck off.'

'I have to collate the VFD engineering data for Kris by tomorrow.' Merlin paused. 'Have you seen Tristan Grazer's going to be hosting the Fantastic Journey series for NatGeo experiences?'

'Should I know who Tristan Grazer is?'

'He's the fucking biggest action star on the planet. Do you live under a rock? Don't you read the Tremaine Group news feed?'

'Nope, and I'm not into watching movies or TV,' Enzo paused. 'Take a look at this.' He glanced around the lab to make sure they were alone before opening the program on his Gatekeeper of Dreams unit. He handed Merlin a pair of AR glasses. 'Check this out.' Enzo tapped play on the dreamforming interface.

The scene opened with a muscular naked man chained to the wall of a candle lit dungeon. Two scantily clad women entered, one carrying a bottle of oil. They proceed to oil him all over, paying close attention to the semi-engorged member between his legs. One of the women removed a candle from the wall and held it close to their captive's groin, teasing the clearly frightened man, who had wilted with the threat. Spurred on by her friend, she held the candle to his pubic hair and within seconds the man bursts into flames from head to toe, screaming and writhing in pain.'

Merlin ripped off his glasses. 'You're an evil fuck, Enzo, you're going to hell.'

'I hope so, probably more fun than the other place.' Enzo removed his glasses. 'No, no, no...I didn't author it.'

'Who did?'

'Can't say,' he evaded Merlin's stare. 'Working title is SinTown. You can watch or–'

'You know this sort of shit can get your friend fired on the spot?' Merlin warned. 'We produce experiences that appeal to the masses, not the depraved. Backyard developers will produce this sort of shit, not us.'

'Is the rumour true?' Enzo changed the subject.

'What rumour?'

'That the FH codester training program will be open to anyone soon.'

Merlin didn't want to confirm or deny the rumour. 'Seems you know more than me,' he deflected, before he turned and walked away.

After a few steps, Merlin stopped and looked back at Enzo. 'You tell whoever authored this shit, Saxon knows, cause I'm going to tell him.'

A small door at the side of the room opened, grabbing their attention. Two cleanerbots emerged to begin their duties.

'I think Saxon's got enough on his plate, don't you?' Enzo shut down his unit. 'Home time.'

'Jeremy, Jeremy, Jeremy,' FBI Special Agent Rufus Geiger repeated. 'You keep talking in circles.'

The interrogation room was deliberately humid, stifling. Jeremy Abernathy was lathered in sweat. 'It's strange how time is distorted when you're doing something you dislike,' he contemplated. 'Thirty minutes on a treadmill feels like forever, yet four hours at a party flies by. I feel like I've been under your warm and considered care for a week, but it's only been days.'

'You know, I have a feeling too, Jeremy, a feeling you'll be suffering our hospitality for some time yet.'

'You forget, I have...'

Special Agent Salim Hasan entered the room and whispered to Agent Geiger. They both looked at Abernathy.

'Jeremy Douglas Abernathy,' Agent Geiger began, 'you are being extradited to Australia for aiding and abetting in the kidnapping of Hugo Zynn and Christine Knox. Stand up.'

'What? What are you talking about? I want my lawyer.'

'You can speak to your lawyer on the way to the airport, now get up,' Agent Geiger said.

Agent Hasan grabbed Jeremy by the arm and forced him upright.

'You can't fucking do this! I didn't have anything to do with a kidnapping in Australia,' Jeremy protested as the flexicuffs were applied.

On their way to Hawkins Field Airport, Jeremy attempted to contact his lawyer several times, but the connection failed.

'I must contact my lawyer before I get on that plane,' Jeremy stressed to the agents.

'You've had an opportunity to contact your lawyer. The network's congested,' Agent Hasan told him. 'Out of our control.'

A jet waited on the tarmac. The aircraft was signed with the Tremaine Group logo on the tail fin.

'What the fuck?' Jeremy said when he stepped out of the vehicle. 'I'm not getting on that.'

'This aircraft is going to Sydney, and you'll be on it,' Agent Geiger assured Jeremy.

'No, I wo–' Jeremy began, collapsing from the jab administered by Agent Hasan into the side of his neck.

Agents' Geiger and Hasan dragged Jeremy's limp body to the stairs of the plane, where they were met by two men, who continued the boarding procedure.

The agents watched as the jet taxied across the tarmac to the runway.

Jeremey Abernathy slowly came around. Walt Tremaine sat opposite him in the plush aircraft cabin, staring at him. 'Abernathy, meet Waylon Devereux.'

Jeremy flicked the man seated next to Walt a quick glance before he tested the restraints fastening his arms. 'You can't fucking do this, Tremaine, this is abduction.'

'How does it feel to be on the other end?'

'I had nothing to do with your grandson's kidnapping you fucking fossil!'

'I'd like to believe that. But the authorities think otherwise.'

'There are rogue elements, zealots who are part of our congregation, I admit that, but I don't condone their actions and I have no connection to them. I'm disgusted by what they've done.'

'We just want Hugo and Christine back safely, then we can all go about our business,' Walt said.

Jeremy struggled in the restraints. 'You might think you're the almighty, Tremaine, but believe me, when this is over, I'll destroy you.'

Walt gave him a faint smile. 'More powerful men than you have tried to destroy me, Abernathy, I won't hold my breath.'

'God will smite you, Walter Tremaine, mark my words.'

'Fuck your god. I have a plan for you, Abernathy.'

'I'm sure you have.'

'Suicide,' Walt threatened.

Jeremy looked anxious. 'Fuck you. You might think you're God–'

'God? I'm no fictional character.' Walt turned to Waylon, 'See what this man knows.'

Waylon waved over two men to untether Jeremy.

'You can't do this, Tremaine!' Jeremy warned again, as he struggled against the substantial henchmen dragging him to the back of the cabin. 'You can't fucking do this!'

'Oh, but I can, Jeremy. Where's your fucking God now?'

Three recruits followed Merlin from the lab elevator.

'Wendy, I'd like you to meet our codester newbies. This is Iminka Korhonen, Arrow Wagner and Liam Ho.'

Nods and smiles were exchanged.

'Good morning and welcome.'

'Wendy wears a couple of hats as our lead in computational sociology and as a neural code engineer,' Merlin announced.

'Today you'll be experiencing dream immersion,' Wendy explained. 'As a trainee you need to experience it before you can author it.'

'I've got a tasty little experience called Hitchcock's Half Hour,' Merlin said. 'It's a thriller named after Alfred Hitchcock. You heard of him?'

Iminka, a heavily inked young woman, shook her short cropped blonde head.

'Master film maker known for the mood he created in his films. His strong visuals conveyed menace without the use of graphic violence or much dialogue,' Arrow said.

'An aficionado, Arrow?' Merlin asked, impressed.

'My grandfather loved his films, we used to watch them together.'

'Yes, he was a master film maker from the early to mid-20th century.' Merlin picked up a DI dashboard. 'Users normally select their own experience and preferences for immersion, but today I've done that for you. Your timecode will be displayed on your arm and you'll have just over 30 minutes to explore. Ready?'

Liam and Iminka nodded.

'Sure am,' Arrow said. 'I've been looking forward to this. Is it as real as I've read?'

'You tell me when you return,' Merlin answered.

'Should we give them a safe word?'

'Nah,' Merlin grinned. 'They've signed on as trainees, they consented to everything.'

'Select a sleep pod and we'll get started,' Wendy instructed before her PD buzzed. She quickly glanced at the text message from Margo. *Just coping. I'll call u l8r. tnx for d tip, dream phaze is gr8 idea 4 ad campaign.*

Daybreak crept up on Liam, Arrow and Iminka as they wandered down a quiet residential street straight out of 1960s USA. The dawn chorus of birds began their song.

'This is very cool,' Arrow said. She noticed the green timecode on her wrist, *32 minutes* and counting down.

'It's spooky. It's so realistic,' Liam commented. 'Can you smell that?'

'Chicken?' Iminka asked. 'Barbecue chicken?'

'Yeah, the whole tangibility...is mind blowing,' Arrow added.

Something on the ground caught Iminka's eye. 'Look at that.' Iminka pointed to a metallic box, adorned with several ruby red stones, sitting in the gutter. She walked over and picked it up. 'It's heavy.'

'What does that say on the lid?' Arrow asked.

'Open only if you are sure,' Iminka read out.

'Sure of what?' Liam questioned.

Iminka went to open the box, but Arrow put her hand on the lid. 'Are you sure?'

'Sure of what?'

'Exactly, then don't open it,' Arrow said. 'We need more information.'

'It's just a box,' Iminka said.

'Do you know where we are or what we're supposed to do?'

'Arrow's right, we need to find out where we are,' Liam agreed.

Arrow took the box from Iminka.

Iminka immediately snatched the box back from Arrow. 'I'm sure I'm not going to let you tell me what to do.' She opened the lid and instinctively let out a high-pitched scream as she dropped the box. A bloody female head spilled from the box and rolled gently to the gutter.

'Fuck that looks real,' Liam said.

A man ran with purpose from the nearest house. 'Are you alright?' None of them answered. 'Are you okay?' he repeated.

'Sure, sure, we're okay,' Arrow said, as she walked over to the head.

The clean-cut man in his thirties did a double take when he saw the head. 'Who...who's that?'

'It was in that box,' Iminka told him, her breathing still laboured.

'I think I'd better call the sheriff.' He turned to go back inside.

'Wait!' Liam called.

'I've never seen you around here,' the man said, turning and sizing each of them up. 'I don't want any trouble.'

'What's the name of this place?' Liam asked.

The man stood silent for a moment. 'Fairvale of course.'

'Are you cooking chicken?' Iminka asked.

'Why?'

'It smells great. Can we taste some?'

The man stared apprehensively at each of them, before he motioned them inside with his hand.

Iminka and Liam walked towards the house.

Arrow remained where she was. 'I'm not hungry. I'm going to look around, I'll be back in ten.'

'Whatever,' Iminka said without turning around.

Liam hesitated, looking back at Arrow. He was in two minds, before deciding to follow Iminka.

The man's eyes were fixed firmly on Iminka. 'Do you want a leg or a breast?' he asked Liam as he closed the door. 'I'm a breast man myself.'

Liam didn't answer.

'You must have been sure, to open the box I mean.' The man smiled at Iminka.

Arrow hesitated as Iminka's now familiar scream pierced the tranquil morning for a second time–but she didn't turn around. 'Whatever.'

Iminka was on her PD, while Liam studied the monitoring equipment as Arrow woke.

'You did well,' Merlin acknowledged. 'Lasted the full 33 minutes.'

'A question,' Arrow sat up. 'How do you tell one echo from another? I mean, in the literature you gave us it explained them, but in reality, or should I say in dream immersion, you can't tell if they're elevated, assembled or live? Every human looked real.'

'There were only three live echoes in that experience, two of them exited very early,' Merlin said, flashing a grin at the pair. 'There were two elevated echoes, Lena and Zen. Did you meet them?'

'I did, Zen is crazy, I liked her.'

'The rest of the cast were assembled echoes. We've added timecodes on the wrists of all human form echoes after a recent incident, so live echoes don't standout. There is a way to tell echoes apart, but we'll get to that later.'

'The experience was so authentic, so lifelike, far beyond what I expected,' the twenty-something admitted. 'I don't know why, but I was sort of half expecting that tired old film cliché of short, fragmented sequences with vignette or blurred effects–'

'Too damn real for my liking,' Iminka interrupted.

'That was the point,' Wendy said. 'Now that you know how it feels, how it looks, how real it is, it allows you to author better experiences.'

'For all I know, I could still be in dream immersion,' Arrow added.

'You're not,' Iminka said flatly. 'Can we get on with it, Merlin?'

Merlin considered Iminka. 'For the next six months you'll be living and breathing FH code. Let's go.'

Saxon tapped his PD buzzing on the table as he and Margo ate breakfast in the courtyard of their house, overlooking majestic Sydney Harbour.

Walt's image beamed out from the device. 'Firerock have questioned Abernathy, he gave them nothing. He's in Sydney and agreed to contact the kidnappers to negotiate.'

'Has that happened?' Saxon asked.

'A couple of hours ago. Firerock monitored all the communications between them and they have a good idea where they're being held.'

'Where?' Margo asked as she came around to Saxon's side of the table.

'Canberra. A Firerock team are in the area now. I have to keep moving. I'll get James to call you if there are further developments.' Walt disconnected.

'Are we flying to Canberra?' Margo asked, returning to her breakfast.

'With the media watching our every move? Not yet. We should have a bag packed, ready to go at a moment's notice.'

'At least something's happening, I feel like we're moving forward,' Margo consoled herself.

Saxon's PD buzzed again. 'Mrs Freudenstein?' He tapped the PD interface. 'Hello, Mrs Freudenstein.'

Mrs Freudenstein's projection appeared. 'Hello, Dr Zynn.'

'What's happening? Everything okay?'

'Mr Nembo isn't well today, he's not in the office. He asked me to call you about a couple of issues,' she paused. 'Dr Kilroy wants the FH developer training program open to more universities, and quickly.'

'I know, Kris called me last night. We're losing codesters and we need to replace them asap. I don't have an issue with it, as long as the recruitment procedure remains the same with background checks, psychometric analysis, etcetera. We only want high calibre individuals with solid programming backgrounds,' Saxon explained as he continued to eat.

'Understood. I'll pass that onto Mr Nembo and HR. The second issue is about the bugging of the meeting last week. It seems we don't have a strong case to pursue a single media outlet. The hackers sold the information to multiple media outlets simultaneously, so no single media outlet can be held accountable. The hackers will be prosecuted, but that's where it ends.' Mrs Freudenstein seemed stilted, anxious.

'Are you okay, Zelda?'

'I just feel sick about what you and Margo...knowing what you and Margo are going through with Hugo,' she began to weep. 'Please, tell Margo I'm thinking of you both and my prayers are with you.'

'Thank you, Zelda.'

Margo got up from her chair and came around to re-join Saxon. 'I'm here, Zelda. Thank you for your prayers and support, we need all we can get at the moment.' She took the device off the table and walked inside.

Saxon contemplated his wife as he continued to eat his mushrooms and scrambled eggs. He remembered her absolute joy when she found out she was pregnant with Hugo. The news of his imminent arrival came at the right time in her life, months after her own mother's death, drawing her out of her depression.

Margo walked back out into the courtyard and stole a mushroom from Saxon's plate. 'You have a voice call on hold.' Margo handed over his PD. 'I'm going to pack a bag.'

Saxon looked at the number but didn't recognise it. 'Hello?' Dead air crackled.

'Saxon?'

He instantly recognised her voice. Memories flooded back of her face, her hair, the way she held herself. 'Amanda?'

'I'll get straight to the point. As you are probably aware, the FBI are interviewing Jeremy in relation to your son's kidnapping.'

'Yes.'

'I just want to assure you Jeremy had nothing whatsoever to do with it. The Fundamental Purists don't kidnap, we just don't do that sort of thing.'

'You do in Australia,' he told her firmly. 'Have you been emailing me?'

'Emailing you? No, I don't have your email address. What–'

'If you or Abernathy can help secure the release of Hugo and Christine, do it, and do it fucking quickly.' He disconnected, staring at his device for a moment, before walking over to a small plastic pot plant and kicking it as hard as he could. Shattered fragments and soil flew in all directions.

'Who was it?' Margo asked through the screen door.

Saxon turned, not realising Margo was there. 'Just somebody that I used to know,' he replied.

'Are you alright?' She came out into the courtyard and held Saxon's hand. 'I'm getting calls like that too. People I haven't heard from in years.'

'I hate this fucking feeling of not being...not knowing how to find Hugo. What if Abernathy's not behind it?'

'His fucking cult have got something to do with it.'

'I suppose so,' Saxon said.

'You saw the video.' Margo grew a little suspicious. 'Who just called?'

Saxon remained silent. 'Amanda Voss,' he answered softly. 'She said Abernathy has nothing to do with the kidnapping.'

Margo dropped his hand and sat down at the table. 'Can we believe her?'

Saxon joined her at the table. 'I don't know. It could be a smoke screen.'

'Why didn't you want to tell me she called?'

He gave her a sideways glance. 'I don't want you to worry any more than you need to.'

Margo stood and walked over to Saxon, putting her hand on his cheek. 'You're a good man, Saxon. Better text Dad about her call. Will I throw some things in a bag for you?'

'Thanks, and I'll text Bob to have the aircraft ready to go.'

In Port Augusta, Kris was just getting up. He wandered from the bathroom to the kitchen and turned on the coffee maker. When he turned around, he saw it. The note resembled a lone cloud floating in the middle of the sky-blue kitchen bench. He stared at it for some time before he sat down on a stool. The coffee was ready, so he poured a mug. Finally, he picked up the note.

'My Darling Kris,

I've been trying to work through the issues, but I miss my family, my friends, the buzz of the city hive. I know I haven't been supportive. You know how I feel, isolated out here in the middle of nowhere. You have your work, I don't. I've tried, I can't pretend any longer. I still love you, but I can't live this way and I know you can't do your work anywhere else. Please forgive me.

All my love, Nikola.'

Kris read the note 20 times or more, putting more emphasis on certain words, trying to make it sound better, but it didn't. He poured himself another coffee and walked out into the backyard.

Chapter Seven

Wendy sat in her purple McLaren P1 and Merlin in his black LeFerrari coupe, revving their engines. Wendy turned up the music. *Talking Heads–I'm on the road to nowhere*. Lights flashed red, yellow, green, go!

Merlin exploded off the start line, entering the first corner at 200 kilometres per hour. He passed the first sensor, automatically scoring 600 points. Merlin's vehicle sat low to the ground, engineered to be one of the most powerful performance cars in its day. The carbon fibre design offered minimal wind resistance. It gripped the long, sweeping road in the Italian Alps as if on tracks. Inertia forced his body into the plush leather seat as his lead foot hammered the accelerator. No lag, just adrenaline pumping acceleration and noise. Ferocious V12.

Wendy changed down to take a corner, her McLaren purring, before roaring through the next section neck and neck with Merlin. She pipped him at the next sensor, picking up the 1000 points on offer. Wendy approached the final hairpin bend leading to the freeway on-ramp, smoking her wheels on exit, forcing Merlin through her plume of burning rubber, overwhelming his cabin and nostrils. Wendy's McLaren sneered at LeFerrari as she gathered speed heading for the suite of chicanes.

Merlin ripped chunks out of the road surface, hurtling, sizzling, spitting blue flames. He felt his nerves extend into the steering wheel and throughout the feral beast. Exhilaration. He reached the first chicane, by half a length, and snatched the next 2000 points.

Wendy eased off the accelerator as rain began to fall. Spray from Merlin's vehicle reduced her vision momentarily, making her nervous, unsettled. Out of the chicanes, they raced along the ocean bridge road, 90 metres above the churning water. The rain became heavier. Obstacles randomly appeared along the road and evasive action had her snaking, then briefly fish tailing. The nape of her neck bristled. She felt alive as the sensory overload heightened her awareness. On a wide left bend her McLaren hit pooling water and she began to hydroplane. A bollard obstacle rose from the road, she hit it side on, spinning her car. Adrenaline surged through her body. She hit the bridge barrier with such force her vehicle was propelled over the rail and she plummeted towards the murky water. As if in slow motion, she turned up the music and sang along.

Merlin was oblivious to Wendy's fate as he flicked on the booster and accelerated, another 1000 points won.

At four in the morning, armed mercenaries surrounded a house in suburban Canberra. Dressed in black from head to toe, wearing night vision goggles, the leader gave the order to move in. Three insurgents silently entered the dwelling from the rear, as four entered through the front door. They made their way quietly through the building, clearing each room. The house was empty.

A muffled noise was heard under the house and the search was on for a cellar door. They located the trapdoor under a mat in the second bedroom. Cautiously, they opened the hatch and descended the stairs with weapons poised.

Somebody was strapped to a table, their head covered with a jute sack. One of the team removed the hood to reveal a barely conscious Christine.

Saxon's PD buzzed ten minutes later. 'Walter Tremaine,' the automated voice announced.

Saxon propped himself up on the pillow. He picked up his device and pressed voice call-speaker.

'Walt.'

'They've found Christine. She's doing well.'

Margo was awake and listening. 'What about Hugo?'

Silence lingered in the bedroom. 'No sign of him at this stage,' Walt reluctantly reported.

Margo let out a huge sigh. 'Fuck! Can we speak to Christine? Is Hugo alright?'

'Christine's in no state to talk,' Walt said. 'Maybe later today.'

'It's been a week since Abernathy arrived. Why is this taking so long?' Saxon asked.

'This is the fourth location Firerock have searched, the kidnappers keep moving, but they're getting closer. Once Christine has rested they'll talk to her and have a better idea who we're dealing with.'

'Don't let Abernathy return to the US until they find Hugo,' Margo instructed.

'Of course not,' Walt confirmed before disconnecting.

Saxon rolled over to cuddle Margo. They both remained silent for some time.

'Do you think we'll get him back alive?'

Saxon didn't respond quickly. 'Christine's okay, the signs are promising.'

'You didn't answer the question.'

'I think...the odds are in our favour,' he finally said.

'Me too.'

Later that morning, Wendy and Kris were working in the small developer's lab on level two.

'Are you and Nikola going to the barbeque on Saturday?' Wendy asked.

Kris considered his response. 'No, I don't think so. You?'

'Miranda's in Adelaide for a week, so I thought I might go. Hopefully, she'll bring Michael back with her.'

'Where's your brother been working?'

'He called me from India last week and said he's almost finished his latest assignment and coming home.'

'What's he working on?'

'He's sworn to secrecy. I never know until it's on TV.'

Kris stopped what he was doing. 'Nikola left for Melbourne a week ago.'

'For how long?'

'For good,' he sadly confessed out loud.

Wendy searched Kris' face for a moment. 'How many times has she done this, Kris? She'll be back.'

'I don't think so. The note she left sounded...final.'

The quiet conversation ended when Merlin walked into the lab. 'They've found Hugo's girlfriend, Christine. It's all over the news.' Wendy and Kris stared at him. 'What?'

'What about Hugo?' Wendy asked.

'Haven't found him yet.'

Wendy sighed. 'I've almost finished here. Anyone for a coffee and Spacestix?'

'Count me in,' Merlin said.

'Sure, why not,' Kris said, just before his PD buzzed. 'Have to be quick, I've got a meeting with Alfred about the new codester, I mean developer training program in 30.'

'It's going to be expanded then?' Merlin asked.

'It was just a matter of time. It's arrived earlier than anticipated.'

'Who are you targeting?' Wendy asked.

'Universities worldwide, not just the elite this time. Applicants can either be fee paying students or sit the entry assessment for our trainee program. We'd better get going.'

The three walked towards the elevator. 'So, what happens if we're inundated with paying students? Where do we train them?' Merlin asked. 'We don't have room here at the facility.'

'We don't. That's what the meeting's about, the logistics of running the program in Sydney.'

'Is Saxon okay with that?' Wendy questioned.

'He is. He'll be in the meeting too. We need to think long term so we have a constant bank of developers.'

As they entered the elevator to go down to level four, Merlin explained the experience Enzo had shown him the week before. 'Should I tell Saxon now or wait?' he asked.

'As developers, we all tinker with small, self-indulgent creations–'

'This was fucking dark, Kris, it didn't look like tinkering. Someone has spent serious time on this. Enzo called it SinTown,' Merlin clarified.

Kris looked at Wendy, as if to seek permission.

'You might as well tell him,' she said.

'You might as well tell me,' Merlin coaxed.

'Saxon's aware of foreign orders being authored.'

'Foreign orders?' Merlin questioned.

'Since going public two weeks ago Saxon discovered unauthorised experiences being developed,' Kris elaborated. 'Foreign orders are custom experiences developed for paying customers, written by dodgy codesters using our company resources.'

'Norus diagnostics discovered some anomalies in specific subroutines, so Saxon ran eyes over the platform's indexing PX generator data,' Wendy added. 'He found them and deleted them.'

'Who's writing them?'

'Not sure,' Kris said. 'It's someone who knows the platform very well, they've masked their digital prints. It'll continue to happen, but it's being monitored,' Kris said. 'There will always be certain individuals who push the envelope, it's human nature.'

Merlin shrugged. 'I suppose so. But what I saw was fucking wrong.'

The café was virtually empty, except for the three occupied DI pods. Employees tested dream immersion experiences during their breaks, in return, they had to give detailed feedback on the experiences.

'There's Arrow,' Merlin said. He strolled over as she was waking from the experience. 'How was it?'

'Hi, Merlin.' She removed her DI dashboard and placed it on the holder. Arrow stood up, stretched, and flicked her straight black hair. 'Phenomenal! I'm still in awe of the total immersion, the detail and intuitive nature of the program. I tried Melvin's Maze, the one where you start on the 54th floor of a building and have to escape before it collapses into a sink hole.'

'I know it too well. Did you make it out?'

'No way. I didn't get past the 33rd floor, and that was my third try.'

'Kris and I authored that one, to test a gravity algorithm.'

'It's an adrenaline pumper. I'll try again.'

'There's a trick to getting out,' Merlin suggested.

'Yeah?' Her face lit up. 'Tell me!'

'Join us for coffee and I'll reveal all.'

'You paying?'

'Sure.'

In a Sydney café, the baristabot stood at the machine making coffee as Margo waited. She glanced at the muted 3D wall monitor showing images of Christine and Hugo as scrolling text explained Christine had been found alive and well. She turned away and watched a woman with her tweenaged son. She remembered Hugo when he was that age, an awkward age for him. He was very inquisitive and lived to play 'Shhhhh,' the VR game where the slightest noise attracted the Ripperoos. He would describe in great detail how they attached to your face and sucked the life out of you with circular mouths full of razor sharp teeth. Hugo spent many hours in silence quietly creeping through the 13 levels to gain freedom.

She heard her PD buzz in her bag as the baristabot handed her the cup of coffee. She tapped her earfonic. 'I'm on my way home, just stopped to get coffee,' she told Saxon.

'Walt just called; they have a lead for Hugo.'

'In Canberra?'

'No, Sydney. They want the FBI to release Abernathy before they release him.'

'No fucking way,' she said defiantly. 'I'm heading to the car now; I'll be home in 15.' Margo tapped her earfonic to disconnect. 'Call, Dad.' She waited. 'Dad, don't give Abernathy back to the FBI under any circumstances.'

'Of course not. Firerock have a good idea where Hugo is, they're on their way now.'

'Okay. I'm heading home, keep us posted. I love you, Dad.'

'Love you, Giggles.'

'You...'she hesitated. 'You haven't called me that since Mum's funeral.'

Walt knew the moment he uttered the words, that he hadn't called Margo by her pet name since Sylvia's funeral. 'Haven't I? Sometimes you still remind me of that little girl.'

'Good. I still remember the tickle spider that made me giggle.'

'Me too,' Walt confided with a smile in his voice. 'That seems so long ago, like a different life.'

'It does.'

'I need to...' Walt began. 'Doesn't matter, we'll talk later.' He disconnected.

The low Earth orbit station sat 100 kilometres above the planet. Merlin, Zen and Arrow each sat on their spracers, ready to depart.

'Good to go?' Merlin asked.

'Ready,' Zen acknowledged.

'Yep,' Arrow said.

'After we get going, set your cruise control to 70 k's like I showed you.' Merlin could have eased on his thumb throttle, but he didn't. He squeezed it with determination and accelerated from the platform at speed, the girls following. The cloud mass beneath flashed and crackled with lightning and thunder on their gentle trajectory down towards the show.

Travelling through vast open space above the planet on spracers felt exhilarating. The vista was spectacular. Erupting, engrossing, illuminations grew closer and louder as the trio reached the viewing platform. They dismounted, taking up positions in Acapulco chairs as a waiter arrived with Frog Cutter cocktails for all. Their retinas were momentarily stabbed with electric red lightning sizzling down out of nowhere.

'Fuck!' Zen yelled, spilling some of her drink. 'What was that?'

'A Red Sprite,' Merlin said, as *Morning Mood from Peer Gynt* began playing to accompany the show.

'I've heard about these,' Arrow confessed excitedly.

A volley of massive blue beams blasted up from the gnashing thunderstorm tens of kilometres below, to crescendo in an impressive bank of exploding Red Sprites followed by a bullwhip crack of thunder discharging an intense whiff of nitric oxide.

'Wicked!' Zen shrieked.

'They were Gigantic Jets.'

Their attention was taken by a series of blue-purple tendrils that danced and hissed on the swirling blanket of energy below. Then, hanging in space before them, a pearlescent, glowing curtain of light emerged. One moment it was a single pink ribbon disappearing either end into the distance, the next, it was a multitude of rippling greens, yellows and blues. Expanding and retracting, radiating then fading, the light wall undulated like a living, writhing beast mesmerising its captive audience.

'Aurora Australis?' Arrow asked.

'Based on it, yes.'

'It's beautiful,' Arrow said.

The magnificently choreographed spectacle continued for another ten minutes until it was time to return to the station above.

'You're quite an adept author,' Arrow complemented Merlin as they entered the lounge area of the station.

'Thanks. Believe me, I'm still learning. It takes time to learn the nuances of the program to construct a good narrative, and it's continually changing as other developers add new features.'

'Why didn't you start the experience at the viewing platform, to give users more time with the highlights, instead of starting at the space station?'

Merlin looked at his forearm readout. 'Thirty seconds to exit. The journey to the payoff is all part of the experience. Riding a spracer through open space is one of the subtle differences I'm talking about, the detail that creates a good experience that people will invest time exploring. Of course we can't do any of this in reality, no oxygen and -80°c, we'd be dead. Add space motorbikes and tropical attributes and it creates an interesting storyline. I've created over a dozen variations on this experience changing music, colour, sound effects and visual chorography.'

'I'm still coming to terms with the tool menu,' Arrow admitted.

'You've only been here five minutes, give it time. It took me four months to finish my first project.' He turned to Zen. 'See you soon.'

'Next time guys,' she replied with her infectious smile.

'Bye, Zen, it's been fun,' Arrow said. Her environment blurred to red before fading to black.

Back in the lab, Arrow and Merlin took off their dream immersion equipment.

'If you don't mind me asking, what happened to Zen, to become an elevated echo?' Arrow asked.

'She had a congenital heart disease, and died in that lab,' Merlin said, nodding towards the developer's lab.

'Whoa. Was she your girlfriend?'

A smirk flashed across his face. 'No, nothing like that. She was an admin intern, only here for three months, she was just...unlucky.'

'I really like her, she's good value.'

Merlin smiled. 'Yep, she's all that and a bag of chips.'

'Huh? How fucking old are you? My grandfather used to say that about things he liked too.'

'I'm older than I look.'

Arrow smiled. 'Can I ask a favour?'

'Depends.'

'As you know, orientation week is almost over and we're assigned a mentor to shadow for the next few months. Can I ask you to be my mentor?'

Merlin felt awkward, a little uncomfortable. 'Unfortunately, I'm not one of the mentors, Arrow. The codester's below us, on level three, take on that role. I think you've been assigned to Sterling Lindquist, he's our best developer.'

'Just thought I'd ask.'

'It's always worth asking. If I could be your mentor, I would.'

Christine stirred. Heather, her mother, sat obediently by her bed watching. She stroked her hand as Christine gradually regained consciousness.

'Hello, darling,' Heather said.

Christine tried to speak. She pointed to the water on the tray in front of her. Heather held the glass as she took a sip.

'Where...where am I?'

'Barton Private Hospital. You're safe now, baby.'

'How long have I been here?' She sniffed. 'I hate the smell of hospitals.'

'It's antiseptic. Since early this morning. How do you feel?'

'Tired. Where's Hugo?'

Heather hesitated. 'We don't know darling. The men who rescued you said he may have been taken to Sydney, that's where they've gone.'

Christine searched the room through dark-ringed, disorientated eyes. 'Can I have your PD?'

'PD? Why, darling?'

'Can I have it?' She waited. 'I want to check something the kidnappers said.'

'There's a man outside who wants to ask you some questions about them,' Heather explained handing her the PD.

'I can't tell him much. I was drugged and had a fucking sack over my head most of the time.' Christine tapped the interface of the device. 'Is Dad here?' She handed the PD back to her mother. 'Jeremy Abernathy hasn't been released. The kidnappers said they want him released before they'll let Hugo go.'

'I'll get your father, he'll be so excited,' Heather said as she stood up.

'I'm really tired, I think I might sleep for a bit longer.'

'Of course, darling.' Heather sat. You and the baby need to rest.'

Margo paced the living room, listening to the buzz tone through her earfonic. She picked at the already chipped nail polish on her fingers.

'Margo?'

'Hello?'

'Waylon Devereux from Firerock,' the American said.

'Hi. Any news on Hugo?' Margo stood still.

'We've isolated a house in Ashfield. The team are gearing up to go in now.'

'At last. How's Christine? You do know she's pregnant, don't you?'

'We do. She's still recovering. I don't think she'll know much; she was probably sedated most of the time. The medical staff have given her the all clear. She'll come good in a couple of days.'

'She wasn't...raped?'

'No, no, nothing like that.'

'Thank goodness. Can I speak with her?'

'I'm in Sydney at present and Christine's in a private hospital in Canberra. Her parents are with her.'

'Oh, of course–of course you are. I'll give her mother a call.' Margo couldn't think of anything else to say. 'Call me as soon as you have word about Hugo.'

'I will. I have to go.'

'Thank you, Waylon, for all your work so far. We appreciate it.'

'Glad to be of service.' He disconnected.

Saxon was in the study working as Margo marched in.

'Waylon from Firerock said they're about to go in.'

Saxon stopped his work on the computer. 'Did you speak to Christine?'

'Still recovering. Her parents are with her.' Margo paced anxiously. 'He could be home tonight...no...of course not. He'll have to get checked at the hospital as a precaution. Did you call Peter?'

'Peter's on standby if we need him.' Saxon got up and walked over to her. Her pacing ceased with his embrace. 'Breathe. It might be a few hours before we hear anything.'

Her mind chatter was relentless as he held her.

Chapter Eight

The graveyard shift was well underway when Wendy arrived. Beside a bell and a lantern, an old man and a teenage boy sat among graves in the cemetery. Each was huddled under a blanket trying to fend off the gentle rain and night chills. Four lengths of string emerged from four freshly covered graves and all were tied to the bell.

'New worker, eh?' the dirty faced youth asked Wendy.

'Yep. What do we have to do?' she asked timidly.

'They sent a fuckin' split tail,' the unkempt old man with few teeth said. 'Didn't they tell you?'

'Not really. Just said I'd be experiencing life in 1768 London.'

The old man and boy looked at each another confused. The bell rang once and then again.

'Get the lantern,' the man told the boy. 'You,' he directed at Wendy, 'grab the shovels.'

The boy jumped up and held the lantern beside the bell to see which of the strings was moving. He gently picked up one piece and followed it to a new grave. 'This one, Tom.'

'Quick, get shovels over 'ere,' Tom ordered Wendy.

Wendy watched as the boy and Tom began to dig, scrape, and work with purpose to quickly remove the fresh soil that had become mud.

'Get on your knees girl, and fuckin' dig,' Tom insisted.

Wendy gingerly dropped to her knees and began to take handfuls of dirt out of the hole that was forming.

'Faster, or we'll lose 'em,' the boy added.

The mud was proving to be a worthy opponent, sliding back into the hole. The wooden casket was relatively shallow in the ground and within a few minutes they had reached it. Tom used his shovel to tap on the casket lid. A faint tap could be heard from inside.

'Is someone alive in there?' Wendy asked, disbelievingly.

'Hurry! Get the mud out,' Tom said.

Wendy, soaked from head to foot and covered in mud said, 'This is not entertainment.'

The bell rang again. They all stopped and looked.

Wendy remained on the sleep pod for some time when she returned.

Kris went over to her. 'Are you okay?'

'Yep. Just thinking about the experience. I tested one of the Fact or Fiction experiences. It was intense. Not my idea of entertainment but engaging none the less.'

'I experienced Viking history last week, which was an eye opener.'

'Do you know how the sayings "saved by the bell" and "dead ringer" originated?'

'Erm...saved by the bell's an old boxing term isn't it?'

Wendy laughed. 'Probably.'

Saxon watched from a window as the nondescript white van pulled into his Vaucluse driveway late in the afternoon. Four media drones obediently stationed outside the gate also observed the arrival. The drones transmitted images back to their masters, stalking from afar in warm offices. Long shadows stretched across the manicured lawn at the centre of the circular driveway.

Waylon Devereux alighted first. Two of Waylon's men escorted a third person in a black hoodie from of the van. Underneath the hoodie, a head sack restricted knowledge of the outside world. They led the visitor into the house.

Saxon and Margo were settled in their chairs at the dining room table as he was ushered in and seated. Jeremy Abernathy's head sack remained in place.

Jeremy Abernathy sniffed. 'I can smell salt air; we must be near the ocean.'

'We want Hugo returned,' Saxon told Abernathy.

Abernathy said nothing, letting the silence loiter. 'I want to go home.'

'Not until Hugo's safe,' Saxon said.

'I have to be released before they'll release him,' Abernathy explained.

'You'll tell them it will be the other way around,' Saxon explained. 'Once Hugo's released, you will be released.'

'I've been negotiating for his release since I fucking got here. Someone's obviously tipping them off, like a few days ago. So, until you find that person, we're wasting our time.'

'We want you to try harder. We'll give them an incentive to release him.' Saxon paused, looking at Margo before continuing. 'Give them your word you'll get the dream immersion project closed down for good, then they release Hugo, then we release you.'

'You'll do that? For good?' Abernathy questioned.

'I give you my word,' Saxon promised.

'Who the fuck are you?'

'Saxon Zynn.'

Abernathy broke the silence. 'I don't deserve to be treated like this. I have had nothing to do with your son's kidnapping.'

'We will do what we need to ensure our son is returned,' Saxon justified. 'These are your people; you have some responsibility.'

'So you'll shut it down just like that?'

'They have our son and we want him back. Yes, I will shut the project down,' Saxon repeated.

'I want to see your face. You could be anyone for all I know.'

Saxon and Margo looked to Waylon.

'No,' Waylon stated firmly.

'My name is Margo Tremaine. My husband is telling you the truth.'

Jeremy Abernathy took his time to respond. 'You are giving me your word I'll be released?'

'You have my word,' Saxon reiterated. 'You tell them we'll close the project down, then we'll issue a media release to back you up. The moment we have Hugo, you'll be freed.'

'Okay, let's do it,' Abernathy agreed. Waylon motioned his men to stand Abernathy up.

'For what it's worth, I give you my word, I have had nothing to do with kidnapping your son.'

Margo clutched at Saxon's hand as her heart raced. His eyes offered reassurance as the men walked Abernathy out of the room back to the van.

The next morning, Merlin sat in the lab about to prick his finger with a lancet when Wendy and Kris entered.

'Are you sick?' Wendy asked.

'Don't feel the best. Just checking.' He punctured the tip of his left pinkie then smeared the blood droplet across the sensor on his PD and waited.

'No virus detected,' Merlin's PD reported.

'Great,' Merlin said relieved, cleaning his PD sensor with a tissue. 'Heard the news about Golden Ox?'

'Shmeat?' Kris asked.

'Chindia Food Group have been shut down and the directors jailed. All their products have been taken off the shelves.'

'Why?' Wendy asked.

'Not sure, watch.' He unmuted the monitor.

'–carried out over the past four months have revealed shocking evidence alleging the Chindia Food Group, makers of premium shmeat brand Golden Ox Neomeat, have been using human meat in their product,' the reporter said.

'Disgusting!' Wendy declared.

'Fuck! How many times have I eaten that stuff?' Merlin gagged.

The reporter continued. 'Two of the four investigative journalists have been found dead, reportedly murdered in the past 24 hours. They have been identified as Arjun Ramaratharian from England and Michael Setri from Australia.'

Kris and Merlin turned to Wendy.

'Fuck,' Wendy said quietly, the blood draining from her face.

'Sorry, I...I didn't...I didn't know,' Merlin stammered trying to turn the monitor off.

'No. Leave it on!' Wendy ordered.

The report continued with rough, found footage. 'Undercover footage shot by the murdered journalists filmed the process from start to finish. Children and homeless people living on the streets of major cities throughout China and India were given food and money by female "recruiters". Enticed by the promise of more, the victims were then transported to isolated, high security facilities in the Jiangjin district of western China and the eastern state of Assam in India. The unsuspecting individuals were fattened up on special protein shakes, before being euthanised and finally butchered. The human meat was blended with actual sheets of synthetic meat to produce the once highly regarded Golden Ox Neomeat brand and sold in fashionable restaurants worldwide–'

'Shit, Wendy. I'm so sorry,' Kris offered, touching her hand.

'Shhh!' Wendy insisted.

'It is estimated that 100,000 children and adults have disappeared over the past year alone from city streets in India and China,' the reporter revealed. 'Authorities in India and China have announced they will join forces to investigate the entire shmeat industry which is dominated by these two heavily populated–'

'That's enough. Turn it off, Merlin,' Wendy said, before she reached for a stool and sat.

Kris and Merlin looked at each other, dumbfounded.

'Why didn't someone contact me, to tell me?' Wendy questioned with a trembling lip, before tears rolled down her cheeks.

Kris hugged Wendy. 'The media don't care about relatives.'

Wendy's PD buzzed. 'It's Miranda.' She left the two men and went into her office.

'Fucking harsh way to find out,' Merlin commented.

'It is. I'll call Saxon and Margo,' Kris said, walking up to his office.

The alien landscape was littered with smooth blue outcrops against canary yellow sand. The red graphene exoskeletal frame stood five metres tall and shone in the morning sun. Merlin, snuggly fitted in his mechatronic machine, was getting reacquainted with the exaggerated movements of his extended limbs when he caught a glimpse of the alien. A lone Yux saw Merlin and began its march towards him. Without thinking, Merlin's instinct was to flick his arm towards the humanoid creature, releasing the harpoon weapon. The phallic-shaped barb pierced the belly of the three-metre Yux with ease and protruded from its back. The head of the tethered projectile sprang open into a four-pronged grappling hook that Merlin used to drag the still writhing, screeching beast towards him. When close enough, Merlin grabbed the alien's head in his impressive mechanical hand and crushed its skull like a warm, fresh egg. Merlin ripped the gold tongue from the mouth of the deceased Yux and added it to the trophy band around his upper arm. That brought his tally to 14.

The death screeches from the dying Yux alerted his tribe. Merlin counted half a dozen creatures emerging from the quagmire as he repacked the harpoon. What he didn't see, were the four Yux behind him. Two grabbed his arms while the other pair severed the flex hoses powering his exoskeletal legs, felling Merlin to the warm sand. One Yux raised a trident spear above its head to end Merlin's game, at the moment Zen arrived.

'About fucking time!' Merlin called.

'Sorry.' She sprayed the four Yux with her acid gun, instantly melting their flesh wherever it hit. 'I was ambushed down the hill.'

The wounded Yux retreated as more rampaging aliens reached the pair. Merlin tried in vain to scramble out of his armour, while Zen released her razor-sharp homing disc. The high rotation weapon sliced through the legs of the remaining Yux before it returned to its receptacle in her metal composite suit. Zen crushed the heads of the writhing Yux, putting them out of their misery. She twisted off the gold tongues from each creature and secured them in her trophy band.

'Watch out for the...' Merlin began, but it was too late. The sand collapsed beneath Zen's machine giving her no time to escape.

'Game over. Look, here come mum and dad,' was the last thing Zen said before she was swallowed by the landscape.

Merlin glanced over his shoulder. 'I'm balls deep in trouble...adult Yux.'

Kris was in the small developer's lab later that day when he received the text message.

*'To all staff. Zynn Communications and the Tremaine Group will **not** be releasing the Dream Immersion Platform and will cease development of the technology as of midnight tonight. We will release a media statement shortly. Thank you. Selma Thurston, Operations Manager, ZynnComm Public Relations.'*

He thought for a moment before contacting Saxon. 'Is it true? Are we closing the project?'

'It's not a choice Margo, Walt and I took lightly, but Hugo will always come first.'

'Of course, Saxon, I completely understand,' Kris empathised.

'I know this is a tremendous blow to everyone, but we had no alternative,' Saxon said. 'There are other projects we can carry on with.

Which reminds me, McTavish wants a meeting regarding the Rapid Sun project.'

'The memory recording research?'

'It may get the green light now. Can you set up a meeting in the next day or so?'

'Will do. Wendy's flown to Adelaide to arrange the return of Michael's body and his funeral.'

'I spoke to her about half an hour ago. Bloody dreadful business,' Saxon replied. 'I told her to take as much time as she needs.'

'She doesn't have any other family, Michael was the last,' Kris remarked solemnly. 'The team themed experiences crew will be disappointed; they were scheduled to show us the prototype game this week.'

Silence punctuated the conversation.

Saxon lowered his head. 'I'm sorry, Kris. I have to go; I've got another call.' Saxon disconnected. He checked the number. 'It's Waylon,' he said to Margo putting him on speaker. 'Waylon.'

'They'll release Hugo near Circular Quay after the media statement is released at three o'clock. Once we have Hugo we'll take him to Sinclair Private Hospital. Selma Thurston has organised a couple of media groups so Abernathy can make his public statement. The US authorities have maintained their silence on Abernathy's whereabouts so few know he's in Australia. We've cleaned him up and put him in a new suit and given him a backstory.'

'The news is breaking now,' Margo told them, watching her device.

'I'll be in touch,' Waylon disconnected.

Thirty minutes later, Waylon and his team shadowed an old blue sedan through the Sydney CBD. The vehicle turned into Loftus Place heading towards Circular Quay. Pulling over near Customs House, a thin, gangly Hugo alighted from the rear door. With rapid military precision, the white Firerock van pulled up in front of the sedan blocking it. Waylon and two armed subordinates rushed the vehicle and surrounded it.

Waylon opened the driver's car door. 'Get in the van, now.'

Two nervous young men spilled out either side of the vehicle.

'Don't shoot, we were just following orders,' the bearded driver said.

'Shut up and get in the van.' Waylon pointed at a petrified Hugo. 'You, with me.'

Waylon opened the rear door to a waiting white sedan. Hugo obediently got in.

Saxon picked up his buzzing PD and read the text. 'Waylon has Hugo and he's safe.'

'At last!' Margo exclaimed hugging Saxon. 'Where is he?' Tears trickled down her face.

'At the hospital.'

'Come on,' Margo said, already out the door.

When they arrived at the hospital, Waylon was waiting in the foyer.

'Is he okay?' Margo asked eagerly. 'Can we see him? Which room is he in?'

'Peter's checking him out now. He seems fine.' Waylon said offhandedly.

Saxon read his expression. 'What's wrong?'

Waylon hesitated. 'Let's go into the waiting room.'

In the empty waiting room, a muted 3D monitor on the end wall gave the room a welcoming, less sterile ambience. Margo and Saxon stood, waiting for Waylon's explanation.

'What's going on? You're worrying me, Waylon,' Margo said.

'Please, sit for a moment.' Margo and Saxon reluctantly took a seat. 'We have a... situation. Hugo doesn't want to see you.'

'He what?' Margo was taken aback.

Saxon stood. 'Why would he say that? He doesn't have that option,' Saxon snapped angrily.

'He's ashamed–'

'What? Ashamed of what?' Margo questioned.

'Let me explain,' Waylon said as Saxon returned to his seat. 'When Abernathy first arrived we instructed him to contact the local leader of the Fundamental Purists. We sent her a message from Abernathy to be sent out to all local members asking the kidnappers to make contact via a secure online VPN chat room. They did, thinking we couldn't trace them, but we could up to a point, and that's how we found them each time. We had our suspicions about how they kept one step ahead of us. We've been liaising with Christine's parents, as with you, and we discovered Christine's PD was popping up on the network for a minute or so each day. Heather Knox had been texting Christine, without our knowledge, telling her we were about to rescue them. Heather never got a reply, but she never stopped texting either. It became apparent after questioning the two men we apprehended with Hugo, that Christine masterminded the kidnapping.' Waylon paused, letting the information sink in.

'This is ludicrous,' Margo said.

'After Christine was found, she even used her mother's PD in hospital to alert them we were about to storm the Ashfield house. They said she was behind the emails from Scarlett Drummond too. She's quite devious, and I suspect delusional.'

'Are you sure about all this?' Saxon questioned, somewhat sceptical. 'Why the Scarlett Drummond emails?'

'Hugo corroborated their story. Graham and Zhou, her accomplices, said Christine thought the emails would rattle you. She's secretly been a member of the Fundamental Purists for the past two years, but the name Christine Knox doesn't appear on any of their membership lists. Her alias, Kristine Skarbek, does. Graham and Zhou are both members and admitted being behind the local abductions in recent months along with Christine, targeting dissenting ex-members. Christine then hatched this plan and targeted Hugo. It was so simple; we over analysed the situation. I'm sorry.'

Stunned by the information, Saxon wondered why Hugo would undermine the work he had spent the last decade of his life perfecting? 'I don't understand–'

'Why would Hugo do this to us?' Margo finished her husband's question as she began to weep.

'He didn't consciously plan it,' Waylon said in Hugo's defence. 'He really thought he'd been kidnapped until just after the video was posted. That's when the men dropped the act and Christine took charge. Then she persuaded him to go along with the kidnapping hoax, and he said he felt conflicted.' Waylon received a message through his earfonic and glanced at the wall monitor. Jeremy Abernathy was delivering his media statement live. He attempted to turn up the sound with a wave of his hand, but nothing happened. Realising it must have a remote control, Waylon scanned the room, found it and increased the volume.

'–to deliver the good news that Hugo Zynn has been found alive and well,' a well-groomed Abernathy announced. The onscreen graphic read, *Live Sydney, Australia.* 'I've been in Australia at the request of the FBI and Australian authorities to help negotiate the safe release of Christine Knox and Hugo Zynn and now my work is done. There are rogue elements in every organisation and it is up to us, the leaders, to maintain the flock, to weed out those bad elements for the greater good. My church, our church, the Fundamental Purists has never condone kidnapping, it's against the law. The perpetrators have been caught and will receive the justice they deserve,' a hubris Abernathy paused.

'Let me take this opportunity to congratulate ZynnComm and the Tremaine Group who have promised to abandon their offensive Dream

Immersion Platform. Had they continued with this evil technology, chaos would have prevailed, it would have opened Pandora's box. The sheer audacity of this technology, of engineering dreams, of manipulating our thoughts, is beyond what our God intended. Today we are living longer, we have more leisure time, but we are wasting our lives on the trivialities of instant gratification. We should be–'

'Enough of his shit, mute it please,' Saxon requested. Waylon obeyed.

'Our son is somewhere down the hall and we can't fucking see him. How is that right?' Margo complained, yet again attacking her fingernails.

'How did Christine manage to orchestrate all this?' Saxon asked, still coming to terms with the situation.

'She studies digital media production and her two collaborators study computer science. Technically, it's not rocket science.' Waylon placed the remote back on the table where he found it. 'They never planned on hurting Hugo. Do you want to press charges against Christine and her crew?'

'Wouldn't we have to press charges against Hugo too?' Saxon questioned.

'Not necessarily,' Waylon suggested. 'He was under the impression he'd been kidnapped.'

'Is she even pregnant?' Margo probed, hoping that was a lie too.

'Unfortunately, that part is true,' Waylon confirmed.

'Of course she is, she was the honey in the trap.' Margo stood and paced the room, regaining her composure. 'We can't let this go beyond the few people who know about it,' she said to Saxon.

'There are positives from this,' Waylon offered them. 'Hugo's safe and he wasn't harmed. It doesn't usually end this well. At this point in time there are eleven people on the planet who actually know what happened: us, Walt, Hugo and Christine, Graham and Zhou, and three of my men. I give you my word the Firerock personnel will never speak of this incident. So that leaves Hugo, Christine and her crew. We can clean this situation up if that's what you want.'

'No one is to get hurt,' Saxon stated firmly to Waylon.

'Understood. That leaves a two-part solution, the guarantee of no prosecution and money.'

'What about Abernathy? Won't he talk?' Saxon asked.

'No. He wasn't told anything we didn't want him to know. Abernathy has been well looked after, Walt made sure of that, so he'd sign a non-disclosure agreement. At this moment he's about to board a private jet back to the US and he's a hero to the public and his followers. He'll be on chat shows across the globe in the next few days furthering his cause.'

Saxon and Margo considered each other. They knew damage control was necessary to keep this crisis from going public, from ruining Hugo's life and the project.

'Go in and tell Hugo there will be no repercussions from any of this, but we want to discuss it,' Saxon told Waylon.

Waylon looked at Margo for confirmation, she nodded her agreement. He went to leave, but stopped, picked up the remote and handed it to Saxon. 'Walt's about to give the green light to the project.'

They both turned to the wall monitor. Saxon unmuted as the interview began in the lobby of a hotel.

'–glad Hugo and Christine were found safe and well.' The screen graphic read, *Live Tokyo, Japan*. 'I would like to thank my friend Jeremy Abernathy who agreed to be part of our team. Although we don't see eye to eye on some points, we worked together to focus on what was important, to get Hugo and Christine home safely.'

'Is one of those points the Dream Immersion Platform?' The reporter pursued.

'I'm here to tell you unequivocally the Dream Immersion Platform will be rolled out as planned. We have had to take measures publicly to gain the release of Hugo, but that's behind us now. Dream immersion is go. We've expanded our trainee developer program to include paying students and we'll be creating many new storylines for our Lucid network ready for the worldwide launch in December.'

'Do you think the Dream Immersion Platform will be a success given the stop-start announcements of late?'

'I think it will have the greatest impact of any media technology yet developed. Each leap of civilisation grew off the back of the generation before,' Walt hyped. 'Now we are priming the next generation. It took film, the personal computer and VR time to establish an audience while innovators, entrepreneurs and creators developed new ways to use those technologies. Today we have a much more tech savvy audience, who have been excited about the huge potential and benefits of dream immersion from the get-go. Our neurotech convergence will be much more than an entertainment medium–'

'Mute it. We need to keep this situation locked down,' Margo declared as she tapped her PD interface. 'I will be gatekeeper.' Her forthright demeanour instantly dissolved and transformed to modest gratitude. 'Hi, Selma. Yeah, thanks, the best news in the world. Listen, I need you to run point on the media circus surrounding this situation. Tell them nothing, run every little detail past me and I'll write all media releases. We want our privacy, then when the dust has settled, we'll negotiate interviews. Okay?'

Waylon entered the waiting room.

'I have to go. We'll talk later, thanks, Selma.' Margo disconnected.

'Hugo has agreed to see you.'

'About fucking time,' Margo said. 'We need to keep you and your team on hand for a little longer, Waylon, to keep the media at arm's length.'

'At your disposal, Margo.'

'Where's Christine now?' Saxon asked.

'Here in Sydney, with her parents,' Waylon confirmed.

'Have you discussed her orchestration of this fucking lunacy with her or her parents?' Margo asked him.

'Not at all, we've told them nothing.'

'Good. We'll keep them in the dark,' Margo plotted. 'I'll meet with Christine tomorrow. Where are...err...Greg and–'

'Graham and Zhou? In our safe house.'

'Have the police spoken to them?' Margo continued.

'The police have left us alone on this,' Waylon disclosed. 'Walt had a chat with the commissioner.'

'So the police don't know what's happening, the media are clueless–'

'What are you thinking?' Saxon asked.

'Can you relocate Graham and Zhou with a Nukoin incentive?' she asked Waylon. 'Get them a job outside the country?'

'Of course, anything is possible,' Waylon assured them. 'We can delay the aircraft that Abernathy's on and have them out of the country tonight.'

'No, I don't want them to see or speak to Abernathy, organise another flight. Give their families a damn good cover story too,' Margo ordered. 'Which room is Hugo in?'

A man in a dark coat and cap sat at a table in the dimly lit bar sipping beer, watching Kris as he entered. Kris lent on the bar, gazing up at the neon sign above the shelves of liquor, *Welcome to Dangerous Minds*. He took careful measure of the décor, horror movie posters from the 1960's, 70's and 80's. The mood was gloomy, characterised by the depressing song playing in the background–*Psycho by Beasts of Bourbon*. At the far end of the room the ceiling sloped down and both walls curved in, leading to a single yellow door. Along the opposite wall to the bar, a pool table surrounded by gaming machines was the only entertainment in this dismal place.

'What's your poison?' the grotty, unshaven bartender asked.

'Whisky, straight up.' The bartender measured out the portion by eye then left. Kris speculated what this experience would be about. He didn't have to ponder long.

'You want some action?' the man at the table asked.

Kris wandered over to him. 'Enlighten me. What sort of action?'

'Girl, boy or anything in between?'

'Erm, for what?' Kris teased.

'Don't fuck with me or–'

'No, no, I didn't mean to...okay, a girl,' Kris finally said.

The man pointed with his thumb over his shoulder at the yellow door. 'Go in and turn right.'

Kris peered at the door. 'Open it and go inside?'

'And turn right for girls,' the man continued. 'Black, white, Asian, blonde, redhead, brunette. Whatever tickles your fancy.'

Kris stared at the door for a moment, deciding what to do. 'How much?'

'Depends on how nasty you want to get.'

'Nasty?' Kris suddenly felt uneasy.

'Go and have a look,' the man encouraged with a sly grin. 'Maybe you just want to dip your wick. It's up to you.'

Kris drained his glass and placed it on the table. He approached the yellow door circumspectly.

'Wait!' The man called. 'You'll need this.' He held out a mask. 'Remain anonymous, yeah? Your wife might be in there. Worse still, your mother or daughter.'

The thought disturbed Kris, looking sternly at the doorman as he accepted the black Venetian mask. Turning the jade door handle, he warily opened the door. He bristled as distant screams bounced and echoed down narrow halls. He peered straight ahead into a dark passage, then left, then right. A near naked teenage boy ran into him, the impact knocking the boy to the granite floor. Kris offered him a hand up, but the boy spotted the mask in his other hand and recoiled.

'Leave him be,' a morbidly obese man wearing nothing but a white mask warned Kris as he approached. 'He's mine.' The man paused, panting heavily.

Kris could smell stale perspiration and beer wafting from his bloated body.

Grabbing the trembling teen by the wrist, the man dragged him back from where they had come.

Kris dropped his mask on the floor. 'Rumpelstiltskin,' he said quietly, before vanishing from the experience.

The sizable Federation style house was nestled in a quiet, leafy cul-de-sac. Hovering media hounds loitered lawfully at the front gate.

Margo sat in the vehicle waiting, trying not to pick at her freshly manicured nails. She studied Christine as Waylon escorted her from the house down the stairs to the car. An attractive girl, who knew it.

'Where's Hugo?' Christine asked as she got in and sat opposite Margo.

'Resting at home,' Margo answered with a smile.

Waylon sat beside Margo as the door slid shut.

'I thought Hugo was going to be here, I wanted to see him.'

Margo ignored Christine. She touched the console to opaque the vehicle windows, denying access to the media vultures circling their vehicle eyeing their next meal.

'I just wanted to have a private chat, woman to woman.'

'So what's he doing here?' Christine asked boldly.

Margo looked at Waylon. 'He is my insurance.'

'Insurance for what?'

Margo ignored her again and continued. 'You're an extremely beautiful young woman Christine, I can why my son was attracted to you.'

Christine adjusted her skirt. 'Thank you.'

'I don't know what you hoped to achieve from all this.' She paused. 'I'm well aware of what you've done over the past weeks as Kristina Skarbek with the Fundamental Purists. I know you sent my husband emails masquerading as Scarlett Drummond–'

'I don't know wh–'

'Shut the fuck up!' Margo screamed.

Christine shrank into her seat, clearly disturbed by the outburst.

Margo took her time to recompose herself. 'We know that you concocted this hoax and lured my son. I am concerned that you're pregnant with my son's child, and I don't think for one moment you would be a fit mother. So, this is what's going to happen. You will not be prosecuted for the hoax. Your parents won't be told of your actions. After all, you are an adult and you make your own decisions, however twisted they are. You will be paid 20,000 Nukoin to remain silent on this matter, and of course, you will terminate the pregnancy.'

Christine remained silent and still.

'You will sign a non-disclosure agreement which also states you will terminate the pregnancy within one week from today. Sign it and I'll transfer half the funds immediately. The other half after you confirm the termination.'

Waylon handed Christine a document.

'And if I refuse?' Her tone was brazen.

'Graham, Zhou and Hugo have recorded statements implicating you as the architect of the hoax,' anger crept into her voice. 'You'll go to prison for many years. Your choice.'

Christine sized both Margo and Waylon up. 'Do you have a pen?' Waylon handed her a pen and she signed the document. 'I never wanted the little bastard anyway. Hugo begged me to keep it,' she admitted candidly.

Margo's steel gaze remained fixed. 'Of course you didn't.' Margo tapped her PD and then handed it to Christine. 'Enter your bank account details.'

Christine added her information. 'I got what I wanted.' She handed the PD back to Margo with a winner's grin.

Margo touched the transfer key. 'The funds are in your account. Stop the car,' she directed. 'I suggest you move, re-establish yourself. Never discuss what you did with anyone, or my friend here will find you.' The car pulled over and Waylon opened the door. 'Never contact my family again. Get out.'

Christine calmly stepped from the vehicle looking smug. 'Nice doing business with you.'

'Nefarious cunt,' Margo muttered under her breath as the car door severed their brief, yet significant encounter.

Chapter Nine

Psychedelic fluid patterns splashed, exploded, dissolved across the station walls. Arrow quickly jumped on the burnt orange single monorail car as it slowly departed, disappearing into a dimly lit tunnel.

'I was wondering what happened to you,' Merlin said. 'I thought you must have changed your mind.'

'Hey, girl,' Zen greeted.

'Hi, Zen.' Arrow sat beside her. 'How have you been?'

'Fine.'

'I got delayed,' Arrow explained to Merlin, then paused. 'What do you think of Sterling?'

'Sterling's a slippery sucker. He's a crack codester but a fucked human being.'

'Don't get me wrong, I've only worked with him for a week, but...' she screwed up her face. 'There's just something erky about him. I've swapped with Iminka, she seems to like him.'

'Peas from the same pod those two.'

'So, what are we doing today?' Zen asked.

'My major project for the traineeship,' Arrow told them. 'I wanted to start early and I wanted you two to be the first to see it. It's just a taste, the first few minutes, with the working title Surreal Feast.'

'I liked the station,' Zen said.

The monorail car emerged from the tunnel opening into splendid daylight as the old classic tune by the *Eurythmics–Sweet Dreams are made of this*, faded up.

'Wow! Zen exclaimed. 'This is weirdly beautiful.'

'You're a Dali fan,' Merlin commented.

'Isn't everyone?' Arrow responded. 'I'm yet to add work by Kay Sage, and Bosch, Morski, Ernst.'

Dali's wife, Gala, hovered naked above a flat rocky outcrop, sleeping. A bee buzzed around a pomegranate and an elephant with colossal, elongated legs wandered the countryside. The monorail passed under enormous, distorted bodies then snaked around a larger than life 'Lobster telephone'.

'The composition's exquisite, Arrow,' Merlin remarked. 'Everywhere you look there's something odd, other worldly–'

'I love the red roses floating like clouds,' Zen said.

Melting watches and sleeping heads propped up with sticks littered the landscape. Eggs, burning giraffes and above them, an all-seeing eye in the sky were evocative representations of Salvador's quirky style.

'I've always liked how surrealists explored the complexities and imagery of dreams to try to understand the subconscious mind,' Arrow explained. 'I thought this experience was a natural fit for what we do.'

'Indeed it is,' Merlin agreed.

On the drive to the airport, Saxon saw the first billboard with the new slogan– *Are you going to dream phaze tonight?* The words vanished as the next advertisement appeared. 'Where did dream phaze come from again?'

'Originated online, it's slang for engineered dreams,' Hugo answered without looking up from his PD. 'Don't you have someone monitoring social media?'

'She's sitting beside you,' Saxon countered with a grin.

'Wendy suggested we use dream phaze,' Margo added. 'Perfect phrase to reboot the campaign.' Margo checked her PD. 'The ads have been running 24 hours worldwide and dream phaze is trending at number one.'

'Can I?'

Saxon turned his attention to Hugo. 'Can you what?'

'Dream phaze tonight.'

'Are you 21?'

'No.'

'Then no. You'll be denied access until you're 21,' Saxon told him.

'You must have a fix for that, a work around for family,' Hugo pressed.

Saxon looked at Margo. 'Can you believe this guy?'

Margo shrugged. 'Can you?'

Saxon considered both of them. 'The cell age analysis code is meshed within the operating system as a safety precaution.' He paused searching for an analogy. 'It's like the bootup firmware when you turn on your PD. If it doesn't pass all of the runtime services during initialisation it won't start up, it won't start the operating system. The cell age analysis protocol has a similar function, if cell analysis fails, dream immersion startup stops. It's not a bug you can fix or bypass.'

'So, I'll take that as a no,' Hugo said facetiously.

'I'll tell you what. When we get to the facility you can try to dream phaze, okay?'

'Sure, we can do that,' Hugo said, running his fingers through sandy blonde hair. He gazed out the vehicle window across the sunny Sydney skyline remembering, dissecting the last four days of discussions, of concessions. He felt drained, he felt relieved, but mostly, he felt safe.

Margo's PD buzzed; she had a new voice message. She listened to the message through her earfonic.

'Christine here. On reflection, I think I'll need more Nukoin to re-establish myself. Another 20,000 should do it. Transfer it today and I'll move forward with the termination.'

Margo chipped at the nail polish on her right hand as she pondered. She texted back, *'Only if u meet me @ Templeton's, Anzac Pde, Kensington @ 8 2nite.'*

Christine replied. *'OK.'*

Christine Knox alighted the Southeast light rail car at Moore Park alone and walked across the Anzac Parade overpass. The evening was chilly and the traffic flowed steadily under her. On the other side, she hesitated amidst the constant stream of pedestrians, looking up and down the street for Templeton's. Christine was unaware of the two male police officers who approached her from behind.

'Christine Knox?' one officer asked.

Christine spun around. 'Ye-yes.' A look of surprise flitted momentarily across her face.

'We need you to come with us please.'

With precision, a white police van with lights flashing pulled up on the street beside them.

'What's this about?' Christine asked nervously.

The side door of the vehicle slid open and the police officers shuffled her into the vehicle in seconds.

'What's going on?' Christine questioned before the door slid shut.

The van drove for some time before arriving at a private medical clinic in a northern Sydney suburb. A nurse with a wheelchair waited in the drop off zone of the driveway. The two police officers removed a sedated Christine from the vehicle and placed her in the chair. She was wheeled inside by the nurse as the police van slowly departed.

That same evening, Margo lounged under the transparent dome above their residence at the Port Augusta facility, watching Good Morning Florida on her PD.

'This morning we have Jeremy Abernathy with us,' The interviewer announced. 'Good morning, Jeremy.'

'Good morning, Juan, glad to be here.'

'Let's start with the release of Hugo Zynn and Christine Knox. What was your role in their release?'

'A significant one, Juan. Without me it probably wouldn't have panned out as well as it did for those kids.'

'I understand the FBI requested your help because the kidnappers were members of the Fundamental Purists movement in Australia. Is that right?'

Jeremy squirmed momentarily in his seat. 'Sadly, that is correct, Juan. Let me say, we do not tolerate kidnapping or the deprivation of any person's liberty. There are sinners in any organisation, Fundamental Purists are no different. If there is any criminal activity, any wrong doing within our congregation, we will be the first to weed it out and work with authorities.'

'What happened to the members responsible for the kidnapping?' Juan questioned.

'I believe the Australian authorities are dealing with them.'

'We contacted the authorities in Australia regarding this case and we couldn't get straight answers regarding the whereabouts of the perpetrators. They refused to release any information about the case.'

'Maybe Walt Tremaine knows what happened to them,' Jeremy swiped sarcastically.

'Speaking of Walt Tremaine. How did you get on with the man who funded the Dream Immersion Platform?'

'I may have assisted Walt Tremaine in the safe return of his grandson, but that's where the cooperation ended. To a Fundamental Purist, engineered dreams are a profanity, an abomination. Dreaming is significant for our connection with God. We believe our dreams are a sacred place where we listen to the word of God, be guided by the word of God. This technology trivialises, even mocks how our sermon is delivered to our congregation. That's why we're holding a series of rallies against dream immersion technology across the country, starting this weekend in Los Angeles–'

Margo's PD buzzed as text superimposed over the interview screen. '*Package arrived @ destination safely. W.*' She smiled.

Kurt and Kris stood above the lake, contemplating the bask of crocodiles thrashing about in the murky water below. Monkey Madness, the next challenge in the Xtreme Dream Survivor game, involved climbing across 25 metres of monkey bars suspended 50 metres above the croc infested lake.

'Which level is this, Kurt?'

'Twenty-seven.'

'How many levels have you created so far?'

'One hundred and sixteen,' Kurt smiled.

Two sets of metal monkey bars sat parallel to each other, stretching from one side of the narrow gorge to the other.

'Let's do this,' Kurt prompted.

'Any rules?'

'Nope. Ready? Go!' Kurt immediately leapt up onto his bars and swung from one rung to the next effortlessly, making it look easy.

'Not really,' Kris responded slowly, before he ran, jumped up and grabbed the first rung.

Kurt swung his legs up and hooked his feet around the solid frame then deftly scrambled up and over the side of the bars to the top. Carefully, Kurt stood upright on top of the monkey bars, getting his balance. He took his first step onto the next rung, then the next, and the next. He made quick progress as his courage grew.

'Fuck,' Kris muttered as he looked down, straining with halfway to go. Glancing across at Kurt, the hint of a grin flashed across his face. Kris' hands and shoulders were aching with pain as gravity pulled at the dead weight of his dangling legs.

Kurt reached the other side of the ravine and jumped off onto the ground, ending with a forward roll back up onto his feet. 'Come on, Kris, push yourself.'

Kris stopped dead with about 12 rungs to go. 'I'm fucked,' he panted.

Kurt checked his forearm. 'Twenty-five seconds to exit, Kris, come on.'

Kris' grip weakened. 'I forgot to program my safe word or kill switch,' he admitted as he slipped and hung by his fingers. He fell. 'See you on the other side,' he shouted up at Kurt. 'Rumpelstiltskin!' Kris yelled in vain, remaining in the experience. The leathery reptile's back was hard as he hit, knocking the breath out of him. He bounced off, into the jaws of hungry beasts. Gruesome screams were fleeting as the crocs fought over Kris like he was the last chip amongst a squabble of seagulls.

Kris woke first. 'Being chewed on by crocodiles was an experience I'll always remember.'

Kurt took off his forearm dashboard and removed his earstims. 'You should have climbed on top.'

'I will next time.' Kris took off his DI gear and went over to help Kurt. He moved the portable hoist over to the sleep pod. Kris gathered up the sling loops and secured them on the hoist crossbar. Kurt Stimpson was a tall man, almost two metres. Using the hoist remote control, Kris raised the sling with Kurt safely gathered in and manoeuvred him off the sleep pod, depositing him in his waiting wheelchair.

'How did you like it?' Kurt asked.

'Fucking great if you like being eaten by crocs. I prefer your WWII experience, Resistance. I've played it three times and I still haven't stopped the message getting through.'

'Next time check your safe word is programmed,' Kurt advised with sly grin.

'Certainly will. I've got a lot on my mind at the moment.'

'Heard from Nikola?'

Kris shook his head.

'Xtreme Dream Survivor will appeal to a wider demographic. Oh, I almost forgot. We have to postpone the team themed experiences meeting this week, my crew found some last-minute bugs we need to work through.'

'That's not leaving much time for edits. I'll let Saxon know.'

'I'd better get moving, I've got a lunch meeting.' Kurt accelerated up the ramp to the elevator.

Andrew McTavish was waiting in Saxon's office when he returned from lunch.

Saxon was forewarned he was waiting. 'How are you, Andrew?'

'I'm fine. Welcome back. Must be a relief to have your son back unharmed.'

'Utter bliss is how I would describe it,' Saxon answered with a smile. 'Please, sit. Did we have a meeting this afternoon?'

'We had one scheduled two days ago, but that came and went,' Andrew responded.

'Sorry, I didn't get back to the facility until late yesterday.'

'Of course, of course, you had more important matters on your mind.' Andrew McTavish took a deep breath before launching into his next thought. 'I wanted to touch base regarding, Rapid Sun. We've made significant progress in recent weeks. We've finally deciphered the defragmentation hurdle by employing bioneural psychofractal algorithms and we're ready to proceed to the next stage.'

Saxon considered him for a moment. 'Limited clinical trials?'

'Of course.' Andrew read the expression of discomfort on Saxon's face. 'Come on Saxon, I've known you long enough to know that look. Spit it out. What's wrong?'

'I appreciate your dedication and perseverance, Andrew. Believe me, I do,' he paused. 'The problem, no, the issue I have with this tech is the possible abuse when law enforcement get their hands on it.'

'It's not that different to dream immersion, we simply attach strict rules and access protocols. It's inevitable that memory preservation will be exploited across several scientific fields as well as the commercial sector. New uses will emerge as we test it. Use of uncharted tech territory always evolves that way,' Andrew argued. 'We might get to a stage where we decide to block law enforcement, or the military from using it. I totally understand your concerns, Saxon, but the issues are not insurmountable. Why have I been working these past years if we don't commercialise the tech?'

Saxon stood and wandered over to his office window, gazing out over the sleep lab deep in thought. 'Let's see what the board have to say. Organise a demonstration for our Friday meeting and we'll discuss how we move forward from there.'

'Thank you, Saxon,' Andrew rose from his chair smiling. 'I think you'll be surprised with the latest development.'

'If all goes well on Friday we'll continue to develop the tech, as we explore possible restrictions.'

'Agreed.'

Kris knocked on Saxon's office door. 'Sorry to interrupt. Just wanted to remind you we have our team meeting in five.'

'Just finished, Kris, he's all yours,' Andrew said, leaving the office.

Saxon followed him out. He waited until Andrew was out of earshot. 'I just wanted to check in with you. Is Nikola still out of the picture?' Saxon enquired in a sympathetic tone.

'How did you know?' Kris asked, a little uncomfortable.

'Wendy told Margo; Margo told me.'

Kris evaded Saxon's gaze. 'Yep. I don't think she'll be back,' he answered in a small voice. 'I–I'd better get Merlin,' he stammered, eager to end the awkwardness.

Saxon reached out to Kris, touching his forearm. 'I just want you to know. If you want to grab a beer, or ten, and have a chat, we can,' Saxon offered.

A smile emerged across Kris' face. 'Yeah? After work?'

'Sure.'

'I've invited Sterling along to the meeting, to give us an update on staff overtime.'

At that moment, down in the main developer's lab, Sterling Lindquist was absorbed in the conception space at his developer's station authoring a project. Iminka, a few metres away working at a network diagnostic terminal, appeared pleased with herself.

'Check this out,' Iminka beamed. 'I've created a bubble, partitioned within the Norus network, and I can save experiences there, or anything.'

Sterling paused his project and took off his augmentation glasses. 'What? Are you sure?'

'Look.'

Sterling checked the graphic overlay of the network. 'Have you been detected?'

'Not as far as I can see,' Iminka reported.

'How is that possible?'

'It's called pin-holing. I learnt it from a badhat flatmate in London. I was bored, so I tried it with Norus and it worked. The process allows entry through a tiny data defect and can be expanded like a bubble. It sits within the main network but it's masked, basically invisible, never scrutinised by network protocols. Hidden in plain sight. If you don't know what to look for you wouldn't know it was there. Best thing is, we control it.'

Sterling's PD buzzed. 'Shit, I have to go. The powers above have summoned me to a meeting. This,' he said pointing to the monitor, 'is between you and me, no sharing.'

In the meeting room, Saxon scrolled through projected data files, pausing and studying them.

'How was McTavish?' Kris asked as he and Merlin strolled into the space.

'He's going to present his updates on Friday. He wants to move to trials.'

'When you shut the project down last week and said we were switching to Rapid Sun, I must admit, I was pissed off,' Kris admitted.

Saxon left the files and joined Merlin and Kris at the table. 'I couldn't say anything until the plan was executed.'

'I was devastated, until I saw Uncle Walt telling the world we were back in business,' Merlin confessed with a grin.

'So the Sydney training academy is back on too?' Kris asked.

'An academy?' Merlin questioned.

'Yep, all projects are go,' Saxon confirmed.

'Afternoon,' Sterling greeted and took a seat.

'What do you want to start with?' Saxon asked.

Kris scrolled through screens on his tablet. 'I've been keeping an eye on the foreign orders. I found one I've called Dangerous Minds. There was a live echo participating in it.'

'Kris said you've seen one of these foreign orders too?' Saxon questioned Merlin.

'Briefly. So if live echoes are accessing these foreign order experiences, someone's supplying equipment and access to the network.'

'Correct,' Saxon said. 'We need to shut this down quickly.'

'Absolutely, Saxon,' Kris supported, before he turned his attention to Sterling. 'You have your finger on the pulse, Sterling. What's the juice on the floor? Which codesters are creating foreign orders?'

Sterling remained expressionless under the gaze of the three men. 'Is that what you're calling them, foreign orders?' He casually rolled his head on his shoulders stretching the muscles in his neck. 'Enzo showed me an experience of a burning guy, is that what you're calling foreign orders?'

'That's one alright,' Merlin confirmed.

'Do you know who authored it?' Saxon pressed Sterling, but he remained quiet. 'Was it Enzo?'

'I have no idea,' Sterling answered dismissively.

'You fucking liar!' Kris attacked with venom.

Darting glances were exchanged between Saxon and Merlin.

'I started my career as a cyber forensic analyst–' Kris began.

'We all started somewhere,' Sterling interjected. 'I was a soldier.'

'I did some digging and found the dashboard IP entry point was from one of the beta testing units in the field,' Kris laid it out. 'About 20 minutes before I entered the experience, a text message was sent with network access instructions from the main developer's lab. I checked data traffic and that message came from your PD, Sterling. I checked your developer's station project log and that led me down a rabbit warren of records, falsified evidence that you created to mask your actual data, covering your tracks.' Kris threw his device on the table. 'I eventually found links to you authoring Dangerous Minds. You can't argue with hard data. It's all in there.'

Saxon picked up the device, running eyes over the information. 'Response, Sterling?'

Sterling expelled a defeated sigh. 'You got me,' he yielded without a fight. 'I admit it, I authored that experience.'

'Why?' Merlin was dumbfounded.

'Easy, a bucket of Nukoin,' Sterling replied.

'Good work, Kris.' Saxon placed the tablet back on the table. 'Did Enzo help you with this, Sterling?'

'Enzo? No fucking way. I foolishly showed him and he blabbed to your boy here,' nodding to Merlin. 'I work alone.'

'We anticipated foreign orders, but this is out of hand,' Saxon continued. 'Your days of authoring foreign orders are over, Sterling. This is what will happen. We're going to establish a third division. Lucid will remain as division one for our retail distribution. Division two, Dream Stream for custom business orders, and the third division will be known as uDream, for authoring and delivering custom experiences for paying individuals or small groups–'

'To allow paedophilia?' Kris asked incredulously.

'Of course not,' Saxon opposed. 'Our uDream service will only deliver custom orders using a partitioned part of the network. They will go hand in hand, we author and host, they can't have one without the other. This way we can control content. We're going to turn this to our advantage.'

'Makes sense,' Merlin agreed.

'So you're going to allow experiences like Dangerous Minds where sexual predators prey on children?' Kris questioned.

'No, Kris, that won't be tolerated,' Saxon assured him again. 'All projects and developers will be scrutinised from here on in and experiences must sit within the law.'

'But that's the type of experience some users want,' Kris stressed. 'The sick type this twisted fuck authored. How are we going to stop him from doing it again?'

Saxon considered Kris for a moment before focusing on Sterling. 'This is where you make a life choice, Sterling. You either leave ZynnComm today with nothing, or you stay and develop a strategy to manage the projects and developers for uDream, eliminating foreign orders for good.'

Sterling considered all three men through piercing aqua eyes as he thought. 'I only authored it for the money. If you make it worth my while, I'll stay.'

'Smart man. Correct answer,' Saxon patronised. 'Kris, I'd like you to monitor and scrutinise the new division.'

Kris eyeballed Sterling. 'Gladly, Saxon.'

'Okay, so that's sorted,' Saxon said. He turned to Sterling. 'So, are all the codesters putting in the overtime?'

'There are always one or two that have to be poked, but overall, everyone's putting in.'

'Is that reflected in our project completion rate, Kris?' Saxon asked.

'Absolutely. Based on our projections, project completion is on track.'

'Excellent. I'll come down and see you later, Sterling,' Saxon said.

Sterling remained in his seat for an awkward moment, before realising he had been dismissed. He stood to leave.

'Remember, this conversation doesn't leave this office,' Saxon reminded him. 'Your new position of responsibility requires discretion and confidentiality. If in doubt, speak to Kris.'

Sterling locked eyes with Kris before the trio watched him leave the meeting room.

'Fuck, Kris, that was orbital,' Merlin praised. 'I did not see that coming.'

'Why the fuck would you give that tool a position of responsibility after he authored that revolting shit behind our back?' Kris confronted Saxon. 'And without even knowing where the Nukoin came from?

'Merlin, who is our best codester?' Saxon asked.

Without missing a beat, he said, 'Me.'

'Really?' Saxon prodded.

'Maybe Sterling, or Kurt,' he admitted half-heartedly.

'The greedy arsehole deceived us, but I'd prefer to keep Sterling close by on a tight leash, generating income for us rather than being headhunted by someone else,' Saxon clarified.

'He has a point,' Merlin told Kris.

'Have you checked all his project files for foreign orders?'

'No, that's fucking days of work to sift through. I backed up all the data from his station in case he deletes it—'

'We need to check it. I can help so we don't alert staff.' Saxon offered. 'We need to know everything he's worked on and who contracted him. I'll ask Alfred to personally follow the money. We'll need to check all codester project files.'

Kris' frustration evaporated. 'You're the boss.' He referred back to his tablet. 'Kurt's postponed the team experiences meeting until next week, to address a few glitches.'

'By the way,' Saxon said, 'a heads up about this arseholes exploits would've been nice.'

'And spoil the drama,' Kris grinned. 'I told you he was coming to the meeting.'

Saxon looked sideways at Kris. 'What's next on your list?'

That evening, on Anzac Parade in Kensington, Sydney, just up from Templeton's bar, a police van pulled up with lights flashing. Inside, Christine Knox was roused from unconsciousness with ammonia inhalant. The side door slid open and a drowsy Christine was helped out of the van by the same bogus police officers.

'You're free to go,' one officer said as he checked her eyes, ensuring she was aware of her surroundings. He slung her handbag over her shoulder.

'What?' Christine swayed on her feet, disorientated, looking around. 'Erm...okay, good.'

Both officers boarded the van and closed the door. The flashing lights were extinguished before the police van merged back into traffic.

Christine searched the streetscape, getting her bearings. Unsteady, she began to walk. Her handbag buzzed, so she rummaged through stuff to locate her PD. Blurred vision made it hard to read the text message from her bank–*Funds transfer confirmed. 10,000 Nukoin received.'* Christine was confused. The date on her PD puzzled her even more. She touched her belly.

Saxon and Hugo ate breakfast under their sundrenched dome. Saxon, wearing sunglasses, felt a little worse for wear after his drinking session with Kris.

He considered Hugo for some time before he spoke. 'I haven't asked before, but now we have a bit of time and distance between us and the events back in Sydney, I'd like to know why you chose to stay with Christine during the kidnapping hoax?'

Hugo remained silent, contemplating his response. He rested his fork on his plate, put his PD down, then relaxed back in his chair. A grimace worked its way across his face. 'I've thought about this long and hard because I knew you would eventually ask me. I felt...I felt torn between our family and Christine, and our baby. I admit, I made the wrong choice. I was confused.' He paused. 'At first it was like a wicked adventure, but as the days dragged on, I realised the seriousness of what I was caught up in. By the time Christine decided she wanted to go home because of the morning sickness, I was over it. I had no quarrel with you or your work. I was never part of the Fundamental Purists movement. When it was over I was so relieved. But then the guilt kicked in. I didn't want to face you or Mum because I felt like such a fucking idiot.'

'Thanks for being so candid. It takes guts to admit when you're wrong about something.'

'I'm going to tell you something, just between us, don't tell Mum.'

Saxon gestured zipping his mouth closed.

'When Mum told me Christine terminated the pregnancy I was pleased. I know that sounds harsh, and selfish. That was the longest period I'd ever spent alone with Christine. She's a gorgeous girl, and I thought I was in love...but because we couldn't use our PD's, we had to talk, and have lots of sex of course, because that's what Fundamental Purists do. My little head was doing all the thinking.'

'You poor little bastard,' Saxon mocked. 'Here we were worried sick, and you two were banging uglies like there was no tomorrow.'

'She's quite narcissistic, and honestly, she's got the personality of a lettuce. I think she's a little unbalanced, because of her baggage.' He paused, looking at out across the landscape. 'She told me her father molested her when she was 15.'

'Did she report it?' Saxon asked.

'She told her mother, but her mother didn't believe her. I think her problems manifested from there.'

'That type of abuse would damage anyone,' Saxon concurred.

'You know, this conversation has made me wonder. Maybe that's why I stayed with her, I felt sorry for her. She has no one in her life to rely on, to support her.'

'Possibly, and your cock was making all the decisions.'

Margo marched onto the deck. 'Dad just called from hospital, he's about to go into surgery. He's getting another liver transplant!'

'He mentioned it to me,' Saxon admitted, before he sipped his coffee.

'What! When?'

Saxon looked a little sheepish. 'A couple of weeks ago. He wanted me to tell you, but I refused. I told him it was his responsibility to tell you.'

'Great! So nobody told me. I'm flying to Sydney.' She stormed off.

'You can keep a secret,' Hugo admired.

'Yes I can. But this wasn't really a secret. It was your grandfather not wanting to deal with your mother. She'll say the same thing I told him, stop drinking.'

More than ten thousand obsessed Fundamental Purists cheered and clapped as crowd fluffers primed the Los Angeles faithful in anticipation of Jeremy Abernathy taking to the podium. A chant erupted, 'Je-re-my, Je-re-my, Je-re-my.'

Half a dozen media drones jockeyed for position above the enthusiastic mass while twice as many police drones scanned the crowd. Placard slogans read, '*Dream Immersion=our nightmare*' and '*Get out of our heads ZynnComm!*'

Finally, Jeremy Abernathy climbed the stairs at the rear of the stage to address the throng. He burst through the curtain onto the stage accompanied by thunderous cheers and applause. His image appeared on large screens, beaming live around the world. Jeremey Abernathy threw his arms in the air and absorbed their energy, their adoration, like the religious rock star that he was. His wife, Amanda Voss, followed him and took her seat with the entourage of inner circle minions. The adoring yet obedient crowd hushed as Jeremy gestured for them to quieten down.

'Welcome, friends. Thank you for coming today. One week before ZynnComm releases their abomination, we are here to tell them, we don't want their product, we don't need their product!' Cheers and yells erupted in support. 'We have to be true to the Fundamental Purists Manifesto to protect our beliefs. Saxon Zynn and Walter Tremaine are dancing with the devil, ladies and gentlemen, and they will suffer the consequences. With God on our side, I believe my divine calling is to bring down ZynnComm's engineered dream technology!' Unanimous applause exploded.

In that moment, the back of Jeremy Abernathy's head blew apart from a single RIP bullet, launching him backwards onto the podium floor. Fragments of the same projectile wounded two of his entourage. Amanda Voss charged towards her husband but security guards intercepted her and bustled her off stage. Another pair of security guards grabbed Abernathy's arms and hauled his limp body through the bloody puddle behind the curtains.

Shock, pursued by panic, coursed through the huge crowd while police searched for a gunman on the ground. Overhead, police drones scanned the erratic mob for the shooter.

The SkyGaze media drone flew from the confusion and headed north. A police drone followed, caught up to it and circled the media drone. Descending, the SkyGaze drone hovered over bromate contaminated Brookfield Reservoir. Close to the surface, it exploded into thousands of fragments, scattering debris across the already polluted water. Parts of the craft floated. Most sank into the gloomy depths.

Chapter Ten

Blue sky smudged with yellow clouds shading the horizon made her feel at ease. Wendy lay in the double hammock daydreaming. The breeze was warm with a hint of lavender. A mob of red kangaroo grazed on white grass and pinkberry leaves from the two gnarled trees that supported her hammock. An inquisitive joey bounced over to her and looked up, expecting a pat with its cute, innocent face.

She called this experience, Nothing. She did nothing, she thought about nothing in particular, she wanted nothing from anyone and she gave nothing to anyone. This was her escape from everything, to do nothing. This was the one place where she could just be herself, just be Wendy. On her return from Adelaide, from Michael's funeral, she realised she needed to add something.

Her brother, Michael, rode up on his bike. 'Hey, sis.' He leaned the bike against the pinkberry tree. 'Room on there for me?'

'Of course, Mikey,' she answered with a smile. 'Just be careful you don't tip us out.'

Michael swung his leg up and into the hammock. 'This is awkward.' He wobbled as he straddled the hanging bed.

'No, not like that. Arse first, silly.'

Michael removed his leg from the hammock and turned around. This time, backing into the hammock, he pushed it away. He tumbled over and Wendy spilled out and fell on top of him, startling the kangaroos. The pair lolled on the grass laughing. 'I never have been very coordinated.'

'That's so fucking true,' Wendy agreed. 'Come on.' She got up. 'Watch me.' Wendy turned her back to the hammock and grabbed it with both hands. She planted her bottom in it and swung one leg up, then the other. She wriggled across to allow room for Michael. 'Now you. Do it slowly.'

Michael managed to board the hammock successfully this time.

'Remember when we used lay on the grass in the backyard and watch the butterflies and bees visit the flowers in Granny Lee's garden?' Wendy asked.

'Yep, and the beetles.'

'You...you remember the beetles?' Tears welled in her eyes.

'Sure do. I remember collecting stink bugs off the lime trees and dropping them down the back of your shirt. You used to stink and Mum wouldn't let you in the house.'

'I remember you were a real little bastard sometimes.'

'Remember the time you saved me from the snake hiding under the old fence palings near the chook shed?'

'I do. You came so close to being bitten. I told you to wear your boots, but no, you had to go bare foot.' They swung in silence for a long moment. 'After this we'll go back to the house. There's a get together with Mum and Dad, Granny Lee and Grandpa, Uncle Wal and Aunty Jen and the twins.'

'Cousin Kenny and Michelle?'

'Yep. Look.'

Overhead the performance was about the begin. In flew a multitude of crystal butterflies, bees and beetles of assorted colours and sizes.

'They're beautiful, sis.'

'After a week-long investigation, police revealed today that based on the trajectory of the fatal bullet, the SkyGaze media drone was the likely source,' the TV news reporter explained, larger than life on the massive wall screen.

Saxon and Hugo watched and ate, seated around the kitchen island in their facility residence.

'Los Angeles police have released footage of the SkyGaze drone exploding over the heavily polluted Brookfield Reservoir.' Police drone footage played as the reporter continued. 'Submersible drones recovered SkyGaze debris from the reservoir, most was contaminated and unsuitable for a forensic investigation. The operator of SkyGaze drones, Altitude Media in New York, has released a statement denying any of their drones were at the rally. However, police said an application had been approved by the organisers for a SkyGaze media drone to attend the event. A Mr Robert Singh was named as the registered remote pilot licence holder. Police confirmed the SkyGaze drone remote link had been traced to a Los Angeles address and their investigations are continuing. Back to you, Jim.'

A news anchor appeared on screen. 'Coming up next, we examine the subliminal pseudoscience behind the Fundamental Purists sermon delivery and explore what happens to the religious movement now the driving force and founder, Jeremy Abernathy, is dead. Also, just 24 hours until the Dream Immersion Platform goes live. Where to buy dream immersion dashboards and what to expect if you're one of the lucky early adopters.' Aerial footage showed people lined up, camping outside stores wearing Dream Phaze t-shirts, cheering as the media drone flew past them.

'Can you believe this hype?' Hugo asked, turning to Saxon.

'Blame your mother.'

'I imagine you met Abernathy when he was in Australia?' Hugo asked.

Saxon continued staring at the screen. 'Very briefly.' He cleared his plate from the benchtop. 'I'm flying to Sydney tomorrow for the launch. You want to come? Mum and Pop will be there.'

'Where?'

'The new Dream Immersion Academy at the Norus network facility near Western Sydney Airport.'

Hugo didn't answer as he chewed. 'No, I'm still working on my course transfer application for ANU.'

'They have a good astrophysics department?'

'Yep. Shouldn't be a problem to get in, if I get it finished.'

'I've got to get to work. Last minute details to attend to. Might see you for lunch.'

Hugo nodded.

Alfred and Mrs Freudenstein were waiting in Saxon's office. Mrs Freudenstein started the recording app on her PD.

'Early start for you two,' Saxon said, placing his PD on his desk.

'Much to do in preparation for the launch tomorrow,' Alfred responded. 'Good news on the thalpherycine licences. They have been granted for all major territories under the New York-Munich Biosoftware Convention.'

'By the skin of our teeth. I bet that took a bit of persuading to get it through in time,' Saxon suggested.

'Contacting them every day for the past two weeks, plus a call from Walt helped,' Alfred said. 'All the thalpherycine dispensing units we deployed last week are online and will be activated tomorrow morning.'

'We fly out at eight sharp tomorrow morning,' Mrs Freudenstein advised. 'Try not to be late.'

'Kris and Merlin know?'

'Yes, and Wendy. She returned last night.'

'Advance DI units have been couriered to all media organisations for review and we anticipate the first reviews to appear by tomorrow afternoon,' Alfred explained.

'Are the instructional videos online yet?'

'They'll go live first thing tomorrow morning,' Mrs Freudenstein said.

'Are all the students going to be there tomorrow?'

'Yes, 60 of them,' Alfred confirmed. 'Twenty trainees and 40 paying students. Plus parents, partners, media, corporate guests, etcetera.'

'We'd better go over the schedule for tomorrow, you're going to be busy with speeches, interviews and whatnot,' Mrs Freudenstein suggested. She handed both men a running sheet for the day.

'This is all indoors, isn't it?' Saxon checked.

Alfred and Mrs Freudenstein glanced at each other.

'Of course,' Mrs Freudenstein said. 'Why?'

'Just been watching the Abernathy shooting. Looks like he was shot using a media drone.'

'Most unfortunate,' Alfred said. 'There will be no media drones at the event tomorrow.'

Below on level four, Wendy, Merlin and Kris sat observing the morning café crowd as they went through the ritual of coffee procurement. A subdued mood loitered over their table.

'You stayed up all night to edit it?' Merlin questioned.

'Yep,' Wendy said. 'Had to get it done so I...so I could talk to him again.'

Kris smiled at Wendy. 'I bet it was worth it.'

The satisfied grin on Wendy's face extinguished her dark mood. 'Fuck yeah. It was great to see him again. The last time I saw him in the flesh was just after Christmas. I met up with him to give him his present,' She paused. 'He didn't like it.'

'The present you gave him?' Merlin queried.

Wendy laughed. 'No, no, sorry, I'm rambling. That I was back with Miranda for the third time,' she said sheepishly. 'He liked Miranda, but he always told me I could do better. He didn't like me running back to her.'

'You should get some sleep, rest up for tomorrow. It's going to be a full-on day,' Kris suggested. 'Saxon will understand. You know we fly out at eight?'

'Yeah. I think I might go home and sleep,' she yawned.

Kris' PD buzzed on the table. 'Come on, Merlin, we have the meeting with Kurt for the team themed stuff in five.'

'I want to see this,' Wendy said. 'I'll sleep afterwards.'

On level two in the small developer's lab, Kurt and his team, Jinny and Bhang, were waiting around the largest holographic table. Kris gestured to Saxon the meeting was about to start as they walked past his office. Saxon signalled two with his fingers.

'I have to go, got another meeting,' Saxon said. 'Has the paperwork begun for the phase one clinical trials on McTavish's project yet?'

'I'm starting it today,' Mrs Freudenstein answered. 'Twelve-month duration, right?'

'Correct,' Saxon agreed. 'We'll probably have to increase it.'

'The fractal neurochemical facsimile process for preserving memory recordings is exceedingly complex, time consuming and expensive,' Alfred commented. 'In the current configuration, prohibitive for law enforcement.'

'Good,' Saxon said. 'I don't want them using it.'

Alfred was already standing. 'We are in business Saxon. Our research expenditure has to be recovered. I am sure we can simplify the process and reduce costs when manufacturing economies of scale are factored in.'

The three walked out of Saxon's office together.

'Given the track record of many law enforcement agencies around the world, we should seriously consider withholding the tech,' Saxon stated. 'See you tomorrow.'

Alfred concealed his concern as he watched Saxon walk away.

As he entered the lab, Saxon greeted everyone. Wendy got a hug. 'How are you coping?'

'Okay. I'm tired.'

'She's been up all night,' Kris informed him. 'Adding Michael to one of her experiences.'

'You didn't waste any time elevating him,' Saxon said.

'I needed to see him again,' Wendy admitted with a tear in her eye. 'Thanks, Saxon.'

Saxon's expression conveyed his confusion. 'For what?'

'This technology. It's going to bring solace to so many people.'

Saxon shared a warm smile before he turned to Kurt. 'Cutting it fine, Kurt, we go live tomorrow. Okay, dazzle us.'

'Bhang, you want to give us some context for the project,' Kurt directed.

'So, to refresh your memories, the team themed brief was to create a MMDG–massive multiplayer dream game. A role playing game to set the benchmark for the platform,' the thirty-something codester with a blonde man-bun began. 'These experiences are all based on team membership, which will build over time. We've developed three narratives so far, but two are still in beta testing. They'll be ready in three months for the hard launch. First off the blocks is World Obelisk League, or simply Obelisk.' He brought up a holographic projection on the holotable, then expanded the image of an arena with his hands. It was a modern Colosseum-style circular structure with three vertical viewing levels. 'This is the arena. We have several sponsors in mind for naming rights, but for now we'll just call it the arena.' He opened the arena with both hands like a magician revealing a trick. A triangular based black structure sat in the centre of a large, turfed playing field. The walls of the structure were trapezoids sloping inwards. Protruding through the open top was a three-sided red glossy obelisk crowned with a bright yellow dome. The three trapezoid walls of the structure lowered forming three white ramps leading to a duck egg blue platform where the obelisk stood proud. Bhang expanded his hand over the obelisk, zooming to focus on the yellow dome top. 'The objective of the game is to scale the obelisk and hit the yellow buzzer to gain points.'

An open, pod-shaped vehicle on four elongated tank treads burst into the arena. 'This is a defender who is driven by a player.' It spun on its axis before crawling sideways along the narrow arena wall like a scurrying beetle. Two more defenders entered, stopped and elevated the driver pod, shifting onto the tips of their four long tracks, before descending and weaving around obstacles spaced randomly throughout the arena. 'There are three defenders whose job it is to stop...the dodgers.' Six people entered the arena, flipping, leaping, tumbling, running. 'Dodgers have to evade the defenders to slam the obelisk buzzer.' He paused the projection. 'Defenders have comms between them, the dodgers don't. Each defender controls one ramp, which can be raised three metres off the ground level with the platform. One ramp must remain on the ground at all times. Defender's vehicles must never come in contact with the obelisk. All players on both sides have one unique weapon each—'

'How long is a game?' Merlin interjected.

'There are two halves of 25 minutes each,' Jinny explained. 'First half, team A sends in defenders, team B, their dodgers. In the second half they reverse. Nine players per team.'

'The team with the highest points at the end of 50 minutes wins,' Kurt added.

'So, that means whoever plays first doesn't know if they've won?' Saxon questioned. 'And the team coming in will pick up their teammates legacy, good or bad.'

'Correct,' Kurt mimicked Saxon. 'The side playing first will know once their teammates exit and contact them. We'll also have our real world online results and standings which will continually update as games are completed.'

'I like it,' Merlin commented. 'It'll feed real world interest and social media.'

'The league will play Thursday, Friday and Saturday nights at eight o'clock across each of the 25 times zones around the world for 20 weeks,' Bhang continued. 'Winners attract four points, two points for a draw. Then the finals begin and so on. Multiple instances of the game will be played in each time zone during play nights, with training at any other time. Tactics can be discussed in the real world.'

'Are dodgers freerunners, like parkour?' Wendy asked.

'Basically,' Bhang resumed the program. 'Full gravity must be on for all dodgers and defenders.' They watched in silence as dodgers ran, leaped and side-stepped defenders. Only one ramp sat on the ground as a single defender guarded it and the other two fended off advances from dodgers trying to breach the ramp leading to the obelisk.

'That's enough background,' Kurt said. 'You'll appreciate it more if you play. Best to be in-game to learn the tactics.'

'Who manages the game?' Kris questioned.

'Four sideline referees and two drone referees,' Kurt said as he accelerated into the main lab towards the sleep pods. 'Users don't just have to play; they can also choose to be coaches or referees–'

'I take it players can be killed,' Wendy said, following Kurt.

'In a variety of ways,' Bhang answered with too much glee in his voice. 'But dodger teams are allowed two subs.'

'Will spectators be assembled echoes or live?' Saxon asked.

'Assembled to start, until it catches on. Users will probably want to watch before they decide to play. Each half will have a new audience.'

'What's it cost to play?' Merlin asked.

'Membership will be 180 Nukoin per team to enter the league,' Kurt said. 'Enough questions–'

'What's the prize?' Saxon persisted.

'The bean counters estimate revenue from arena naming rights, team entry fees, in-dream and real world sponsorship plus advertising will generate about 400,000 Nukoin. We're offering 200,00 Nukoin in prize money and a real world trophy,' Jinny answered.

'How long before we have professional teams?' Saxon continued.

'Within a year,' Bhang said.

'Who's coming in with me? Merlin?' Kurt was eager.

'I'm in,' he responded quick smart.

'I can't,' Wendy said.' I've just finished one.'

'Kris, you go. I've got a shitload of work to do before tomorrow,' Saxon said.

Kris didn't have to be persuaded. 'Alright!'

Sterling adjusted the hip belt and shoulder straps supporting his ammunition backpack. His MK55 sub-machine pistol dangled by his side, attached via the elastic sleeve feeding ammunition directly from the inside of the pack to his weapon. He picked up the lightweight polymer gun and extended the retractable stock before he unfolded the bicep rest. Shortening the stock slightly, he rotated the bicep rest making it fit snuggly between hand and elbow. He was primed.

Sterling stood in the warm sun behind a shed as machine gun fire was heard in the distance. On the January 28th, 2032, they were east of Dallas, Texas. Word came through his comms earpiece; the targets had entered the kill zone. He was to await further orders.

Ambush orders given before sunrise briefed them of enemy strength, weapons carried, patrol activity, habits and expected arrival time. Two squads of ecoterrorists were leapfrogging each other making their way to the telecommunications tower close to the coal fired power station. All the first squad were now in the kill zone.

Sterling cautiously peered around the corner as he flicked the safety off his weapon. He watched the scout walk into view and prop behind a 44-gallon drum. Sterling's finger gently caressed the trigger with anticipation. The scout signalled his group forward. That's when Sterling saw her. He didn't wait for orders. He raised his machine gun, exhaled and slowly squeezed, expelling a continuous volley of rounds that smacked every part of her body. His shots ignited the ambush firefight, slaughtering everyone in the kill zone.

Several minutes later, Sterling and the Texas State Guard, swept the area checking for survivors. He approached the woman lying in the bloody dirt. Her body armour was no match for the sustained peppering hundreds of bullets exacted. Sterling stood over her, focusing on what remained of her face.

'Is that her?' His platoon Sergeant asked.

'That's her. That's Lena Zynn,' Sterling replied.

Sergeant Sanchez told him to get a photo for the media.

'Why not take her head?'

Sanchez looked at Sterling. 'You're a heartless son of a bitch, Lindquist. Get a fucking photo.'

Sterling checked the time on his arm, five seconds. The landscape turned red.

Sterling remained on the sleep pod for several moments, recalling his exploits as a teenage soldier.

After a decade of research, the Dream Immersion Platform had finally arrived. The combined public launch for the platform and the Dream Immersion Academy, went off without a hitch in Sydney. The launch slogan, *'Dare to Dream Phaze'* adorned the entire wall behind the podium in the Dream Immersion Academy auditorium. Now the media circus had to be fed the catchphrase so it could be regurgitated repeatedly for the next 24-hour news cycle. Four separate media scrums had been arranged in different parts of the complex. Some of the academy students hung around to listen; most were in the cafeteria for refreshments with family and friends.

'Abernathy's assassination was a horrific event; especially given the support he gave us during one of my family's darkest moments. He was a hero to many,' Walt declared to ravenous reporters as he stood on the podium.

'But Jeremy Abernathy was your most vocal critic,' one journalist stated. 'He was organising rallies against the very technology you launched today.'

'This unfortunate situation has both positives and negatives. On one hand his murder was a despicable act, on the other hand, it gave us respite from his persistent vitriol that dream immersion was the end of civilisation as we know it. Abernathy was a complex human being, like us all. May he rest in peace.'

'Mr Tremaine, have you ever heard of Locky Slade, the man arrested overnight for Jeremy Abernathy's assassination?'

Walt glared at the young male reporter. 'It's clear the Purists are unpopular and the public are eager to use our technology. I predict our Dream Immersion Platform will be the number one entertainment medium in 12 months!' Walt boasted.

Across the room, Kris was on the end of more technical questions from reporters.

'–so our brain will save memories experienced in dream immersion?'

'Only if you select that preference before you enter dream immersion. Otherwise, they dissolve like our natural dreams.'

'Can memories be added to dream immersion experiences?'

'No. Memories are constructed of extraordinarily complex synaptic neural code. We can't capture that information yet; we're working on it.'

'Can users be someone else or a younger version of ourselves in dream phaze?'

'Dream immersion is extremely complex. At this point in time, no.'

In a dedicated training lab down the hall, Margo watched as one of the fee paying students, Hadrian Judge, was being interviewed about his expectations.

'–having said that, as one of the paying students, my goal is to work in this fledgling industry once I complete my studies.'

'The fees are quite high, who paid your tuition fees, Hadrian?'

'My older sister,' he replied.

'Why not your parents?'

'My parents are dead, murdered during the Gambaldi incident,' the young man stated matter-of-factly.

The hungry pack fell silent for a moment.

'Do you have a background in coding?' The interview continued.

Margo got word through her earfonic from Selma Thurston. Christine Knox was being interviewed by media heavy hitter, Wagner Hussock. Margo promptly removed herself from the media huddle and found the news feed on her PD.

'–and, Christine, you said you did this in support of the Fundamental Purists, because of the Dream Immersion Platform technology?'

'We did. We wanted to make a statement, to draw attention to this horrible, intrusive technology. Hugo was disgusted, ashamed of his father's work. He was always part of the plan, we planned it together.'

'And you were pregnant with his child?' Wagner pressed.

'Hugo and I wanted to keep our baby, but his mother, Margo Tremaine, was furious. She said if I didn't terminate the baby she would ruin my whole family. I told her I needed time to think it over. I was supposed to meet with her, to tell her I was going to keep my baby, but instead I was abducted, drugged and my baby terminated without my consent,' she broke down and began to sob. 'Hugo and I know the kidnapping hoax was wrong, but no one was hurt. Margo Tremaine had my baby murdered.'

'Why have you decided to tell your story now, Christine?' Wagner asked.

'I felt compelled to after Jeremy was murdered. I need to put the record straight.'

Margo closed the interview on her PD. She tapped her earfonic. 'Are you still with Saxon?' Margo asked Selma.

In the Norus network management centre, the facility data hub, over a dozen systems analysts and techbots focused on workstations scrutinising, evaluating information. The master wall screen displayed all data collated across continental territories. Numerous smaller screens surrounded the main screen, reflecting real-time analytical data feeds from the first dream immersion customers. Saxon, corralled by reporters, was ambushed mid-sentence.

'Dr Zynn, Christine Knox has just admitted the kidnapping of her and your son was a hoax, planned by both of them,' a reporter asserted. 'Were you aware of this, Dr Zynn?'

Selma immediately intervened. 'That will be all the questions for today, ladies and gentlemen,' she announced before she whisked Saxon away, security guards blocking eager media trying to follow.

Margo took control of the situation. She brought the interview with Hadrian to an abrupt end, then shut down both interviews in the auditorium. Security briskly escorted all media from the complex.

Wendy, Kris and Kurt wandered into the auditorium from the cafeteria. 'What's happened?' Kris questioned.

'Christine Knox,' Merlin said, holding up his PD. 'She–'

'Thanks, Merlin. You can watch it later, Kris,' Margo interrupted. 'Mrs Freudenstein, can you alert our flight crew we'll be leaving early. And, Zelda, make sure the bar fridges are fully stocked.'

'Of course.'

Saxon pulled Margo aside. 'Have you spoken to Waylon?'

'He's on it,' she replied. 'He'll have it released within the hour.'

'I've tried Hugo, but his PD diverts to message.'

'I've tried too,' Margo said. 'We'll see him soon enough.'

Jubilation had evaporated from the ZynnComm team, downgraded to a subdued mood.

'In this current onslaught of malicious slander,' Walt guided them, 'never show weakness, never apologise, never explain and never back down.' His pep talk came straight out of the Walt Tremaine business playbook. 'Whatever this young woman has said, it will be old news tomorrow, and we'll continue to roll out the best entertainment platform the world has ever seen.'

'Let's say goodbye to our students and guests and head home,' Margo suggested, herding the group towards the cafeteria.

Three hours later, the somewhat inebriated team stepped off the aircraft in Port Augusta. During the flight, a judiciously worded media release from Margo had denied all accusations claimed by Christine. Shortly afterwards, a carefully edited video of Christine Knox accepting 20,000 Nukoin and spurning her unborn child as a 'little bastard' surfaced, reaching blistering speeds going viral. Christine quickly became old news as Walt had predicted. The launch was back on high news rotation as the public's appetite for dream immersion skyrocketed. Feedback trickling in for the platform was nothing short of phenomenal.

'You boys want to keep this party going back at my place?' Wendy asked Merlin, Kurt and Kris. 'Miranda can cook up some of her famous pork steaks with apple chips and fennel.'

'I'm in,' Merlin accepted.

'Me too,' Kris piped.

'Sure,' Kurt added.

As the team parted company outside the facility hangar, Alfred, Margo and Saxon were last to leave. Alfred beamed as he studied his PD.

'You look like the cat who swallowed the canary,' Saxon said to him.

'I am, Saxon, I am. All eight and a half million units sold out, generating five billion Nukoin or over 20 billion US dollars.'

'Fuck,' Margo said. 'That's a good day at the office.'

'One of the best in my 26 years with Walt,' Alfred admitted.

'Come on you,' Margo said to Saxon, tugging his arm. 'I want to see Hugo. See you tomorrow at the party, Alfred.'

'Thanks for today, Alfred. It's been a long time coming and we couldn't have realised any of this without you,' Saxon praised.

'It was a team effort, Saxon, it always has been.'

Saxon smiled at Alfred before he followed Margo towards the elevator. That's when he noticed the car missing from the car park. 'I don't think Hugo's here, the car's gone.'

Margo stopped and looked across at the empty space. 'Shit.'

Margo put her bag on the floor beside the kitchen island bench, before speed dialling Hugo on her PD. Almost instantly, they both heard buzzing coming from his bedroom. Margo found his PD sitting on the table in his bedroom, on top of a handwritten note.

The shout came from the bedroom.

'Are you okay?' Saxon rushed into Hugo's bedroom.

Margo sat on his bed, furious. 'He's fucking gone. Look!' She shoved the note at Saxon.

'Sorry for bringing so much shame on our family again, at this critical moment in your life Dad. Just to be clear, Christine was lying in her interview. I never said those things about your work and I never planned the kidnapping. I saw your response to her allegations...seems that everyone deceived me. I need to get away for a while. I love you both. Hugo.'

'Where would he go?' Saxon questioned, as he sat beside Margo on the bed.

'Not ANU, his application is there on the desk. Take your pick north, south, east, west. Fucking little shit!' Margo exploded.

'I'll get Waylon on to it,' Saxon went to stand up.

'Wait,' Margo said, reaching for his hand. 'Maybe we have to let him go, let him sort himself out.'

Mind chatter shifted into overdrive as they contemplated that option in silence.

Finally, Saxon said, 'Isn't life funny. You visualise how you think certain days are going to pan out...and then, on one of the most successful days of your life, you finish sitting on your son's bed wondering where the fuck he is. Back to reality quick smart.'

Margo touched his cheek. 'Hugo's a big boy now, he'll work it out,' she paused. 'It's still early...you want to go over to Wendy's?'

Saxon thought for a moment. 'That's the logical option.'

Next day on level three, in the main developer's lab, energetic staff members and their plus ones fuelled by music and alcohol, gathered for the success party. On the benches, equipment had been replaced with an assortment of lavish finger food and an impressive bar. A large holotable sat precariously atop a bench, ready for Walt's imminent appearance to address the troops.

Merlin projected video from his PD onto a blank wall adding colour and movement to the festivities as people waited for the live feed from Sydney to kick in. He paused on a live broadcast from Jeremy Abernathy's memorial service in Aberdeen, Scotland, immediately provoking boos, taunts and jeers from the 160 strong gathering.

'Get that fucker off!' Enzo Fontaine called out.

'Notice there's no aerial footage,' Merlin said to Arrow standing beside him.

'Look, that's Christine Knox,' Wendy said to her partner Miranda, pointing to the image. 'Talking with Amanda Voss, bottom right of picture.'

'Over the space of three hours Knox went from being the Fundamental Purist's pinup girl to her parents disowning her,' Arrow delighted.

'Some girls are just born lucky,' Miranda said with a grin.

'Get him off, Merlin!' Enzo yelled again and Merlin quickly obliged.

Liam walked over to the group.

'Ahh, Liam,' Arrow said. 'Merlin, we have a narrative for an experience we'd like to pitch you.'

'How are you, Liam?' Merlin acknowledged, leaving his PD projecting a music video.

'Better after a few of these,' he said, holding up his beer.

'Okay, tell me a story,' Merlin invited.

'Liam writes sci-fi stories in his spare time, as a hobby, and he gave me a couple to read,' Arrow explained. 'I thought one of his stories could be adapted for a continuing experience that the three of us could create.'

'Excuse my ignorance. What's a continuing experience?' Miranda asked.

'I've told you about this,' Wendy frowned. 'It's a story without an end, the narrative continues. Liam, this my partner, Miranda.'

'Hi, Liam.'

Liam nodded and smiled.

'Got a title?' Merlin asked.

'GalNexus,' Liam answered. 'Short for Galactic Nexus. It's a space adventure, with backstory. It's set in the 25th century and starts around the edge of the Solar system where a beacon's been found. The beacon points to a superspace conduit, a wormhole just outside the Solar system called Garro GalNexus, named after Captain Chica Garro, commander of the Sygnet 2, who found it.'

'Chica? Spanish female name,' Wendy said.

Liam continued enthusiastically. 'On board the Sygnet 3, players enter GalNexus, a superspace corridor, an ultrafast connection to other parts of our galaxy. It's a manufactured, stable wormhole created by the Breemund species. Travelling through GalNexus is where the real adventure begins–'

'I like the idea of a good old-fashioned portal story,' Merlin agreed. 'Even though VR has thrashed it, dream immersion would add a whole new element.'

'Sounds like a solid base for a continuing experience,' Wendy commented.

'Do you want to help out on this, Wendy?' Arrow asked. 'More the merrier.'

'Yeah, sounds like a challenge.'

'Merlin?' Arrow pressed.

'Yes, but we–'

At that moment, Saxon, Margo and Kris entered the lab to cheers and applause.

They each applauded the crowd. Margo gained Merlin's attention and pointed to the holotable. Merlin switched off his PD projection and turned down the music.

Walt Tremaine's projection beamed up from the holotable moments later, overlooking the crowd like a messiah about to deliver the sermon on the mount.

'Can you hear me?'

'Yes!' Came the spontaneous response from the gathering.

'Good, good. Now quiet down you rowdy bastards.' He looked around the room. 'Everybody here? Saxon and Margo?'

'Yes!' The jovial crowd repeated.

'Okay. Welcome everyone to this momentous milestone!' An impulsive cheer went up. 'We've had nothing but massive positive feedback for DI. The entire world is talking about your creation, about our revolutionary technology!'

The crowd erupted with thunderous applause and howls.

'I've always been fascinated and inspired by the capacity of a small group of people with a common goal to effect change for the majority. Today, that has been realised around the world. Of course none of us, I repeat none of us, would be standing here today without the imagination and determination of one man, our genius Saxon Zynn.'

The room exploded with appreciation, cheers and whistles.

'Listen up everyone, please. I'll get this over with quickly so you can all get back to the serious job of drinking and eating, and more drinking.' Walt waited until the mob settled, as a glass of scotch on the rocks was handed to him by someone his end. 'What we're delivering is not some cheap trick. We are literally delivering experiences that people crave. Just in this very short period of time, people are marvelling at the subtlety, the nuances, the meticulous detail in experiences. I was surprised to find out today that dream phaze parties are already a thing! People who bought the hardware are sharing it because they want their friends and family to experience what they've experienced. Human beings are not simple creatures to please, but it seems we've pulled it off. This type of reaction on a global scale is unprecedented. Congratulations everyone on a huge effort; you've changed the world!'

More jubilation surged through the lab as people began to let go and enjoy the fruits from years of hard, tedious work.

'But we have to remain vigilant. In future, once the novelty wears off, it won't be good enough to give users what we think they want. They will keep coming back if they can experience something that no one else has experienced. We all want to be that hero in films, games and novels. That's what we need to offer users, the chance to live out their wildest dreams. Saxon has given us the tech to engineer imagination like never before. When I first entered dream immersion with Saxon I wasn't sure of what to expect. In there, my adrenaline pumped. Why? Because it was an adventure, it was dangerous, but at the same time it was liberating. Once users appreciate that they're in a safe environment they'll push the envelope, even to the point of risking death.

We've set-up a website for the public to make suggestions and vote for new experiences. I want all of you to keep an eye on it, to keep our content fresh as competition heats up. We must stay ahead of the game! Okay, enough of this old man's bullshit. You all know you've made a fucking awesome product, it's time to kick back and celebrate that fact. By the way, there's a 1000 Nukoin bonus for every employee! Cheers!' He held up his glass in a toast before taking a sip.

'Cheers!' the crowd responded, then simultaneously chugged their drinks. Whooping, howling and hollering swept everyone along, morphing into a chant. 'Sax-on, Sax-on, Sax-on, Sax-on.'

'Come on, Saxon, say a few words.' Walt urged, before drinking his scotch.

Saxon stood on a chair and raised his free hand to the rabble. He gazed at the eager faces staring up at him. 'Sometimes, I had my doubts that this day would ever arrive, ladies and gentlemen. But it has. I stand alongside everyone here, just one in a field of many supportive, talented, imaginative, knowledgeable, ambitious individuals who dared to realise this, dare I say it, dream.' Laughter sprinkled with groans followed. 'I would sincerely like to thank that shining beacon of light standing before us, Walt Tremaine, because without his courage, his unwavering support, his steely-eyed vision and his infinitely deep pockets, this project would never have seen the light of day. To Walt!'

'To Walt!' The troops mimicked. Everyone drank, a lot.

After the speeches were over and Walt's image had vanished, Merlin switched on his PD projector. 'I just want to stroke everyone's ego a little more,' Merlin began, 'by sharing my fav headlines from around the world over the past 24 hours.' Screen grabs of headlines began as the small group watching grew. 'Can you see them up the back?'

'No, read them out,' Kurt yelled.

'Will do,' Merlin called back. 'Hello Dream Phaze, Carpe Dream, A True Alternate Reality is Here, The Great Australian Dream, Simulated Reality Like Never Before, Dream Phaze=Time Travel, Dream It! Be It!, DP is Indistinguishable from Reality, Never Stop

Dream Phazing, Sophisticated Tech That Will Change The World, Phaze Craze, The Future is Dream Phaze, Dreaming is The New Reality, 1001 Ideas for Dream Phaze, Don't Just Lie There-Dream Phaze, 24-Karat Gold Entertainment, Lifetime Citizen of Dream Phaze, Dream Phaze is My New Lunch Break, Already Addicted 2 Dream Phaze, August Zuckerberg Wants To Buy Dream Phaze, Dream Phaze Meanz Dream Daze, Dreaming is not just a phaze boys and girls.' Merlin was about to turn the projector off when his eye caught one line of text. 'Look Liam.'

'Travel to exotic destinations in the galaxy and back in just 30 minutes.'

'There's our hook line for GalNexus!' Arrow exclaimed.

Saxon was getting his next beer at the makeshift bar when Alfred pulled up alongside him. 'Did you see the email I flicked you from Cambridge Research Group?'

'Not yet. I finished piecing together the money trail for Sterling Lindquist's foreign order payment.'

'And?'

'It passed through seven shelf company accounts and ended at Santoro. Michael Santoro.'

'The CEO of SanTech?'

'The same.'

'Fuck. That's a handy piece of information to have up our sleeve.'

'Indubitably. What was your email regarding?'

'Oh, the data's in for the 25-year VR longitudinal study. Consumer data showed average usage has increased from two hours a day to six over that period, and convergence-accommodation reflex has damaged both the optic and oculomotor nerves altering midbrain function.'

Alfred stared at Saxon blank faced. 'I thought we already surmised that?'

'We did, anecdotally, and from a few smaller studies. Now we have comprehensive data to confirm it. We can use it in our marketing.'

Alfred finished pouring himself a large gin and tonic. 'Yes we can.' With that he melted back into the crowd.

Saxon turned around and almost bumped into Mrs Freudenstein. 'Sorry, Zelda.'

'I thought Hugo would be here at the party,' Mrs Freudenstein said. 'I haven't seen him in such a long time.'

'It seems he's taken himself on a trip.'

'Where to this time?' Zelda sipped her rum and cola.

'Not sure,' Saxon answered honestly.

'The kidnapping thing, incident, was terribly unfortunate. I'm sorry it happened, Saxon,' she continued, glassy eyed. 'I didn't think it through when I suggested the leak.'

Saxon stared at Zelda, confused. 'What are you talking about, Zelda?'

'You know, when Alfred and Walt were arguing about the project cost blowouts. You were there. Were you there? No...you weren't there.' Mrs Freudenstein was well oiled. 'They needed to get the project up and running, to kick start cash flow because of the investigations in Shanghai and the fiasco in Russia. Walt was genuinely concerned. I suggested the leak–'

'The leak?' Saxon was still playing catch-up. 'What leak are you talking about?'

'The meeting leak, silly.'

Saxon finally put the pieces together. 'You mean Ray Bruce's PD being tapped?'

'Yes. That was my suggestion to fast track the release, to start generating income. Alfred and Walt worked out the detail. I'm so sorry it turned out how it did, Saxon, you know, with Hugo. We couldn't have predicted it would pan out that way.'

Saxon tried to speak, but the words washed around in his mouth, unable to make it past his lips. He stood stock-still, comprehending what he'd just been told. He turned away from Mrs Freudenstein and walked over to Margo. Mrs Freudenstein dissolved into the herd.

Chapter Eleven

The year was 2017. The crowd on the metro platform made it difficult to move. Merlin pushed, bustled his way through the pack of morning commuters waiting for the 7:43 train to Windsor. Sizing each person up, he studied their faces, their body language, their attire. More people entered the platform, ballooning the numbers to three deep from the yellow safety line back to the bench seating along the entirety of the 80-metre platform.

A young woman wearing black stockings, black skirt, cream blouse and black blazer caught his eye. Merlin studied her momentarily, until her mobile phone rang and she answered with a smile and animated conversation. He kept moving along the platform, watching people with their heads lowered as they checked their popularity status on their devices. The digital clock on the wall displayed 7:41. Merlin had reached one end of the platform yet no one stood out. Not enough time to complete one more sweep of the station he thought. He could smell the stale food in the discarded container thrown onto the track, before a putrid fart stung his nose.

As Merlin turned to commence his final pass, a nervous individual standing on the yellow safety line in oversized jeans wearing a weather jacket met Merlin's gaze. The panic-stricken man forced his way into the morning travellers, away from Merlin. Merlin dashed after the man with renewed enthusiasm. He caught the man by the collar, but the man pushed Merlin towards the track. Merlin instinctively redistributed his weight to remain balanced to stop falling.

A warm blast of air preceded the train as it approached from behind. He caught up with the man again. 'Got cha,' he said, pleased with himself. The train was 20 metres away. Merlin pulled at the collar of the man's jacket, only to realise the man had lifted his arms and slipped out of the garment. Spinning around, the man stepped backwards towards the track grinning at Merlin as he fell onto the metal rails. It took seconds to take his life. Every sign along the platform flashed "LOSER: GAME OVER" as commuters stared at Merlin. He checked the green timecode on his arm as the redness swallowed him.

Just after three o'clock, on a hot afternoon, a pair of police officers arrived in an AWD vehicle at the ZynnComm facility hangar.

'Afternoon, officers,' the security guard greeted as he met the vehicle. 'What can I help you with?'

'A vehicle registered to Zynn Communications was located west of Marree, about six hours north of here,' the older officer explained.

'One of ours? What's the rego number?' The guard asked.

'Senior Constable?'

The young officer checked his notes. 'ZC001.'

'That's Dr Zynn's vehicle,' the guard said with a quizzical expression. 'Let me check the vehicle log sheet. Come in.'

The police officers got out of their vehicle and entered the relief of the hangar while the guard went into the office to check paperwork.

'Looks like Hugo Zynn took that vehicle a couple of days ago,' the guard clarified upon his return.

'Hugo Zynn.'

'Dr Zynn's son.'

'Could we speak with Dr Zynn?' The older, spindly officer asked.

The guard strolled back into the office, away from the officers, as he spoke softly into his earfonic. 'The elevator over there will take you to level one. Dr Zynn's wife, Margo Tremaine, will see you.'

Doors opened on level one to Saxon and Margo's much cooler apartment. Margo greeted the officers with an uneasy smile and her hand. 'Hello, Margo Tremaine. What can I do for you?'

'Good afternoon, I'm Sergeant Daniels and this is Senior Constable Tran. A vehicle registered to Zynn Communications has been found west of Marree, about six hours north from here. We understand Hugo Zynn took that vehicle a couple of days ago. Have you heard from him?'

Margo had a gut feeling this visit involved Hugo. 'No. He left his PD in his bedroom. Has there been an accident?'

'No, no. The vehicle was found abandoned about an hour west of Marree. We're following up an enquiry from Marree police who found the vehicle this morning. There's only one pub in town and no one has checked in this week. What was your son doing up there?'

Margo took her time to answer. 'Please, come and sit down. Would you like a cool drink?'

'No, we're fine, thank you,' Sergeant Daniels said as they all sat.

'Hugo's had a rough time lately. He left a note saying he was going away, that's all.'

'We are aware of your family and the turmoil surrounding the kidnapping,' Sergeant Daniels revealed. 'Senior Constable Tran is a huge fan of your husband's technology. He's kept us updated–'

'Have you searched the area?' Margo interrupted, disregarding Senior Constable Tran's apparent adoration. Her intuition stirred.

'Not as yet. We had to establish why the vehicle was there. Joy riders often dump stolen cars once they finish with them. I'll get back in touch with Marree police and get them to search the area around the vehicle.'

'We could fly there now,' Margo blurted out, her mind racing, thinking of worst case scenarios.

Sergeant Daniels let out a nervous laugh. 'Now? Yeah, sure, you can fly up there now.'

'Could Officer Tran accompany us?' Margo thought having a police officer with them would give them more clout.

The two officers exchanged looks. 'Senior Constable Tran?' Daniels asked.

'He can help coordinate the search. I'll tell them to get an aircraft ready.' Margo grabbed her PD. 'My husband will be coming.'

'I don't mean to be rude, Ms Tremaine, but we don't have any information that he's even in the area, he may have hitched a ride to Oodnadatta or Coober Pedy.'

'Sergeant Daniels, let me tell you something about my son. Hugo has a knack for getting himself into strange situations. We have an aircraft and we can be up there in an hour.'

'Could we have his PD?' Sergeant Daniels requested.

'Why? It's locked.'

'PD's absorb who we are, they're our identity. People entrust information to their electronic confidants that they don't share with anyone. They know everything about us. The fact that he left his PD here has me wondering why. Biometric authentication can be disabled.'

'I'll...I'll discuss it with my husband.'

'Which of these is a recent photo of your son?' Sergeant Daniels asked, looking around the room at all the images of Hugo.

Margo picked up one from the table and handed it to Sergeant Daniels. He handed it to Senior Constable Tran who took a photo on his police PD.

An hour and a half later, a ZynnComm aircraft with Margo, Saxon and Senior Constable Tran onboard landed on a desolate, red dirt road in the middle of nowhere.

The group approached two police officers fiddling with equipment in the rear of their police vehicle. The ZynnComm vehicle was parked in front of them.

Senior Constable Tran introduced himself then Margo, Saxon and Abdi Sulaman their pilot, to the two Marree police officers.

'Sergeant Calder. This is Constable Butler.'

'Can you bring us up to speed, Sarge?' Senior Constable Tran asked.

'The vehicle is out of hydrogen. He could have filled up in Marree but didn't. There's no one new in Marree and I've contacted both William Creek and Oodnadatta and no one fitting your son's description has been through there in the last couple of days. The track to Coober Pedy is closed due to a few days of heavy rain last week, so that's out.

He could be in a vehicle on the track between here and Oodnadatta.' The officer paused as he picked up an electronic device from the back of the police vehicle. 'This is the emergency GPS beacon from your vehicle, it hasn't been activated. We've conducted an aerial search of five square kilometres on both sides of the road with our drones, but we haven't found anyone.' He looked towards the western horizon. 'We have about an hour of sunlight left to search. You can use your aircraft to search either side of the track between here and Marree and we'll continue our drone search in the other direction.'

'There's an Air Force base at Woomera. Could we ask them for assistance?' Abdi questioned.

'Sure. We can get a couple of aircraft out of William Creek at first light tomorrow morning too.'

Senior Constable Tran tapped his earfonic. 'Go ahead.' He listened intently. 'Will do.' He disconnected. 'No activity on Hugo's bank or credit accounts in the last few days. I'll contact the Air Force base and see if they can help.'

From sunup to sundown three light aircraft, two police drones and a low-altitude Air Force drone had found no sign of Hugo. After three days, Margo, Saxon and Senior Constable Tran flew back to the facility in Port Augusta.

Red sand stretched to the horizon in all directions as Margo walked, searching. A single sheet of paper caught by the gentle breeze blew towards her. She stopped and watched as it danced closer and closer, before it caught on her shin. Margo read the handwritten poem.

The sun is beating down
As I wallow in the sand
The perspiration gathers,
Drip,
It explodes upon my hand.
My eyes roll back
My voice is lead
My body rock
My god...
I'm dead.

Margo woke with a start.

'You were dreaming,' Saxon said, staring at her. 'You were mumbling.'

'I was?' Margo, disturbed, remembered the poem word for word.

Saxon placed his PD on the bedside table. 'We'd better get a move on.'

Alfred knocked on Saxon's office door before he entered, Mrs Freudenstein followed. Margo sat on the sofa by the coffee table. Saxon's office was as sparse and minimalist like their apartment.

'Good morning,' Alfred said.

'Morning, Dr Zynn, Margo,' Mrs Freudenstein added.

Margo didn't respond.

Saxon gestured to the chairs around the coffee table as he took a seat beside Margo.

Mrs Freudenstein placed her PD on the table and touched record.

'Why have we been summoned this morning?' Alfred enquired casually.

Margo tapped her PD. A moment later Walt's image projected from of the device. She placed it on the table and pressed group call.

Before Walt had a chance to say hello, Saxon began. 'Zelda, you record all your meetings on your PD, correct?'

'That's right, Dr Zynn. I create transcripts of meeting details so I can refer back to them.'

'Zelda told me something at the party the other day that concerned Margo and me, and we want answers,' Saxon stated firmly to the gathering.

'I'm glad you remember, Dr Zynn, because I don't have a very good recollection of that day at all,' Mrs Freudenstein admitted with a smile, not yet reading the tone of the room.

'What's this about?' Walt asked.

'White-anting, Dad. What the fuck were you thinking when you ran with Zelda's fucking irresponsible idea to force us into early product release?'

Alfred stared at Mrs Freudenstein with daggers before he began to speak. 'I do–'

'Shut up, Alfred!' Margo ordered. 'I want you to explain this, Dad. These two lapdogs follow you. Explain this!'

The prickly silence was palpable as Mrs Freudenstein' face withered as she shrank under the gaze of everyone, a tear rolling down her check.

'Well?' Margo pushed.

'Okay. It was an intentional act to get you onside. I was wrong, but we–'

'No fucking buts, Dad! This has got to be the grubbiest act you have ever instigated, cutting us out of the loop, manipulating your own family. Conspiring with such duplicity, with such arrogance with these fucking minions, to get what you wanted. Why didn't you simply come to us and plead your case for early release based on evaporating income and skyrocketing expenditure?'

'Because Saxon wouldn't have–' Walt was cut short again.

'The thing that pisses us off above everything else is the fact that Hugo was dragged into this as result of your stupidity,' Margo ripped into Walt.

'I know, I know–'

'Be quiet! I haven't finished. The fucking unscrupulous manipulation of your own family, your own flesh and blood, for what? More money? Now Hugo has disappeared and there's no trace of him. Waylon and Firerock can't even find him! He's disappeared into thin air thanks to you...you greedy old cunt!' Margo fought back tears as Mrs Freudenstein sobbed.

No one spoke as Margo regained composure. 'This is what's going to happen,' she proclaimed. 'Saxon owns Class A, B and C ZynnComm shares, totalling 40 percent of the company. Tremaine Group owns the remaining 60 percent, but of that 60 percent, I own Class B shares in ZynnComm via my Tremaine shareholding. I was also given Class A shares in ZynnComm back in '41, worth 10 votes per share, when you, Dad, wanted all decision making to remain with us as you raised billions in capital from investors by selling additional Tremaine shares. In the last 24 hours, Saxon and I have leveraged everything we own and then some, to buy two percent of ZynnComm Class A shares from Tremaine, bringing our combined shareholder voting power to 50.8 percent. I'll spell it out for you, Dad. Saxon and I are now the majority shareholders in ZynnComm, and we will be taking control of ZynnComm from today.'

'Hold on there,' Walt protested. 'I'm not–'

'Shut up and listen for once in your life, Dad.'

'Is there a transcript of the meeting with Walt and Alfred about this leaked meeting deception?' Saxon directed at Mrs Freudenstein.

Mrs Freudenstein looked at Walt's projection through wet eyes. 'I was told not to record that meeting.'

'Of course you were,' Margo criticised. 'Alfred and Zelda, your services will no longer be required at ZynnComm, you can go back to Tremaine in Sydney.'

'This meeting is over.' Saxon leaned forward and disconnected Walt as he continued to object. 'Security will escort you to clean out your desks,' he told Alfred and Mrs Freudenstein. 'You have an hour.'

Alfred and Mrs Freudenstein sat shell-shocked. Slowly, they stood to leave. A security guard waited for them by the door.

Saxon and Margo watched in silence as the pair left the office.

Several hours later, Margo had taken up residence in Alfred's old office on level seven. Selma Thurston's projection beamed up from Margo's PD. 'First thing I want you to do as ZynnComm's new Brand Manager is to follow-up The Event countdown banners.'

'Already done. Of the 34 major news channels signed up, 28 have implemented the banners.' Selma reported.

'And the rest?'

'Within the next 12 hours.'

'You're a life saver, Selma, thanks. I should have finalised this weeks ago,' Margo said.

'Don't worry, Margo, I've been keeping an eye on it for you. All the banners will be up and running by tomorrow, it'll be fine,' Selma assured her. 'So you'll be working from the facility now?'

'For the foreseeable future, until I fathom the scope of Alfred's role.' Margo's PD buzzed. She declined Walt's call. A text popped on screen from Saxon, summoning her to level two. 'I have to go, Selma. I'll call later.' She disconnected and headed to meet Saxon.

'Seems to be a one of those days,' Saxon said to Margo as she entered the small developer's lab. 'We need to terminate Sterling.'

'What's he done now?' she asked.

'I've been checking his project files and found this.' Kris handed Margo a pair of AR glasses and pressed play on the Gatekeeper of Dreams unit.

The experience occupied the open space in front of her. She watched as Lena walked into the kill zone wearing body armour, carrying an automatic weapon.

'Is that Lena?'

'Yep,' Kris replied.

As the carnage unfolded, a horrified Margo removed her glasses staring at Saxon. 'Why has he created this?'

'He was there. He was a foot soldier in the Texas State Guard. His platoon ambushed Lena and her squad,' Saxon explained.

'Why...why didn't that come up in his background check?' Margo was surprised by the vile revelation.

'He somehow covered it up,' Kris said. 'It wasn't on his application, or his CV and Jetstone only had a one line entry in their background report. I did some digging and found his State service record. The thing is, he didn't try and hide this experience in his project files, and he knew I was looking.'

'I want to get rid of him today,' Saxon directed to Margo.

'Of course. What are the ramifications?'

'He's one of our best codesters. He's on a new six-month contract, we'll have to pay him out,' Saxon admitted. 'In hindsight, I should have fucking fired him after the foreign order shit.'

'Let's get him in here,' Margo suggested. 'Can you give him a call, Kris?'

'Sure.' He left the lab.

'Have you spoken to Kris yet?' Margo asked quietly.

'I was about to, then he showed me this. Might be better to wait until we've dealt with Sterling.'

Ten minutes later, Sterling joined the trio in the meeting room on level two.

'Déjà vu,' Sterling muttered as he took his seat.

'You were with the Texas State Guard back in '32,' Kris pounced. 'Why did you hide that information, Sterling?'

His confusion was evident as he cast his blue eyes over the trio. 'I didn't hide it.'

'It's not on your resumé or your application form when joined ZynnComm?' Kris quizzed.

'That was in my late teens. It has nothing to do with my programming background when I was hired. It wasn't relevant.'

'You knew Lena and Saxon's relationship when you applied for the position,' Margo accused. 'And then you create that fucking monstrosity of an experience with Lena in it.'

Sterling remained straight-faced. 'Ahh...I knew of the family link, but that wasn't the motivation to create the experience. The experience I created, over a year ago now, was a...' he smirked. 'I knew Lena's elevated echo was in the system, so I accessed it to create an historical experience for our library.'

'Fuck you, Sterling!' Saxon spat. 'You will be escorted off the premises immediately.'

Sterling was confused. 'I was a soldier; I was just following orders. It wasn't personal.'

'Creating the experience was ignorant and debauched,' Kris accused.

'But...but you just promoted me to–'

'Can't you see your position's untenable?' Kris snapped.

'You have no place here,' Margo added.

Sterling's tone changed. 'Okay, fucking be like that. I want my contract paid out, all the bonuses I was promised, plus a 10,000 Nukoin severance bonus, to remain quiet about how and why I was fired.'

'We–' Margo started.

'I tell you what,' Sterling interjected. 'In lieu of any payout, any bonuses, I'll take half a dozen Gatekeeper of Dream units. We'll call it even.'

'You're a feckless arsehole, Sterling. You're not in a position to bargain,' Kris chastised.

'Lick the sweat off my hairy balls,' Sterling lashed out. 'The adults are negotiating.'

In a flash, Kris sprang to his feet and punched Sterling squarely in the face, spilling him out of his chair. Kris' glasses fell to the floor.

Saxon swiftly intervened, holding Kris back. 'You beat me to it you bastard.'

Sterling shook his head, wiping his bloody nose. 'First and last time you ever do that, Kilroy.' His mind squirmed with violence.

'Get up,' Saxon ordered.

'You'll be able to buy units in six months,' Margo said. 'Why do you want them now?'

Sterling stood and righted his chair but remained standing. 'To start my own production company. Six months will give me a jump on the competition. There are plenty of people out there asking for more interesting experiences than ZynnComm is prepared to develop.' He wiped his nose.

'Like your perverted foreign order?' Kris goaded.

Ignoring Kris, Sterling focussed on Saxon. 'There are universal experiences for the masses, and then there are the people in the shadows who harbour more nuanced predilections, demanding more contextualised personal encounters.' He snorted back blood. 'Corporate conscience is a barrier, a nuisance. There's a market for my flavour of entertainment. If I don't do it, someone else will and they'll set the benchmark and make shitloads of money. It might as well be me.'

'You've been contemplating this for a while,' Saxon alleged. 'Have you got a backer?'

Sterling hesitated, 'Possibly.'

'Santoro?' Saxon prodded.

Sterling's quick glance at Kris then back to Saxon conveyed his unease. They knew who paid for the foreign order. 'Michael is one possibility.'

'I don't hold grudges,' Saxon said. The value of his sister's life could not be quantified. 'But I don't lose either. I'll give you the six units once you sign an NDA stating you'll never speak to the media, to anyone about your time with ZynnComm. And...you'll sign a contract giving one of our subsidiary companies five percent share in any company or entity you create exploiting our technology. If you refuse, you'll have no access to our network to deliver your experiences, ever.'

Sterling smiled. 'You're one sharp knife, Saxon, I'll give you that.' He deliberated, weighing up his options. Remembering the camera in the ceiling, he glanced up. 'Let me take one of the codesters with me and you've got a deal.'

'Let me guess, Enzo?' Kris asked.

Sterling simmered. 'Iminka.'

'Okay with you, Kris?' Saxon asked.

'She hasn't finished her traineeship,' Kris responded.

'I'll complete her education,' Sterling grinned with bloody teeth.

'So, as I understand it, this prick gets six Gatekeeper of Dream units and Iminka to create debauched experiences, and we profit from it.' His insolence clearly exposed his resentment.

'We could pay him out and get rid of the scum,' Margo suggested, staring at Sterling.

A forced silence hung in the room.

'From a moral perspective, it makes sense to pay him nothing,' Saxon evaluated, studying Sterling. 'From a legal standpoint, we have to pay him out. From a business prospect, we give him the units and we collect revenue for the foreseeable future.' He paused. 'We can always deny network access if he doesn't comply.'

'Agreed,' Margo said. 'Let's exploit him. He'll always remember us as he watches five percent of his profits disappear each month.'

'Nice to see the dynamic duo in action,' the serpentine Sterling complemented. 'That threat of access will always hang over my head I suppose. So, do we have a deal?'

Saxon turned to Kris, who evaded his gaze. Saxon nodded his agreement.

At 3:14 a.m. Arrow was woken by multiple sirens. The room illuminated with a blaze of dancing coloured light through her window. She found the front door and exited into the yard. The streetscape was changing. Arrow approached the carnival of emergency vehicles blocking access to a massive fissure that had swallowed three houses across the street. Water gushed from twisted water mains as the smell of gas fouled the air and fuelled fires from leaking pipes. Emergency crews scrambled as ghastly screams from inside the cavity panicked distressed residents. A grumbling, groaning ground noise grew.

Arrow stopped. She noticed the edge of the rupture continuing to crumble, growing larger. A police car teetered on the verge of the cleft before it toppled into the rift. Then another emergency vehicle, and another. Screeching timbers begged for help while foundation concrete twisted and snapped as the expanding void consumed another home.

Terrified, Arrow stood frozen on the precipice and stared into the gaping, swallowing wound. The land fell away, isolating her on a narrow sliver. She ran along the fragment of land searching for an escape. It was too late. She watched as her house collapsed into the black abyss around her, below her. More houses, people, vehicles, street posts, trees disappeared into the depths. Then the crashing, moaning catastrophe slowly ceased. Arrow trembled, crouching alone on her flake of ground, the time glowing on her forearm; almost 23 minutes remained. Beneath her, she heard a low, disturbing gurgle. Peering into the chasm, an orange-red glow loomed.

The still night seemed like a fair and necessary juxtaposition to the events of the day for Saxon and Margo as they relaxed under their dome.

'I can't get over the number of secondary products and services Alfred managed to negotiate for dream immersion,' Margo said. 'Designer DI wrist dashboards and carry cases, designer stackable dream pods for shopping centres and airport lounges, DI specific finance for equipment funded by Tremaine Group Finance. He even has so-called experts drafting books! I thought I was good at spin.'

'He always was the go-to man to make things happen.'

'Dad certainly made good use of his talents for their little conspiracy.'

'He did,' Saxon agreed. 'Oh, I forgot to tell you. I spoke with Kris about heading up the DI Academy.'

'And?'

'We discussed the new management structure. I explained you would be taking on the Dream Stream business division and I would continue with RD. He said he would be honoured to run our flagship Academy. He said it would be a great opportunity to nurture the best and brightest. He wants to take Kurt with him as Head Lecturer. I agreed. I told him we were thinking of opening academies in New York and London within the year and asked if he wanted to coordinate all three. Couldn't wipe the grin off his face he was so chuffed.'

'He was so pissed off after the meeting. It was a good idea to wait to tell him. He deserves the promotion and new direction; it'll revitalise him after Nikola leaving. He's been invaluable over the last eight years.

Expanding our training capacity quickly is a natural evolution given the public response and Kris is the right man to do it, I trust him.'

'After I spoke to Kris, I had a chat with Wendy and Merlin and they're happy with their new roles too.'

Margo's PD buzzed. 'It's Dad. Should I take it?'

'We might as well face the wrath and get it over and done with,' Saxon suggested.

'About fucking time,' Walt's gruff voice arrived before his image.

'You needed time to think and cool down,' Margo lectured.

'It was a ballsy move I must admit. Have you been planning this for a while?' Walt probed.

'Only since we found out about the deception,' Saxon responded.

'Well, about that, I just wanted to apologise. I didn't get the chance earlier. I'm sorry it happened; I made the wrong decision. I'm even more sorry Hugo got swept up in it. Still nothing on his whereabouts?'

'Nope,' Margo answered. 'Waylon and his team are still looking.'

'I'm not going to oppose this, erm...uprising. This strategy might be a good move at this point in time. It'll be business as usual as we head towards The Event.'

'I'm glad you're onboard, Dad, because you have no choice,' Margo told him defiantly. 'It was a fucked thing to pull on family. I almost said this earlier, but I held my tongue. You know Mum would have been so disappointed in you, ashamed of you.'

Walt lowered his head. 'She would have, I agree.' He cleared his throat. 'Again, I'm sorry. I just wanted to touch base, to clear the air.'

'Good, so we're all on the same page. Saxon and I will manage ZynnComm from here on with no resistance or interference from you.'

'Agreed,' he responded meekly.

'Good night.' Margo disconnected. 'Old bastard.' They smiled at each other, pleased with themselves.

Meanwhile, Kris sat in his living room toying with an idea. With his PD in his hand, he was poised to send a message to Nikola. *I'm moving to Sydney to manage the new Dream Immersion Academy...the company apartment is too big for one person. Want to play?'* His thumb hovered over the send icon. A knock at the door distracted him, pressured him. His heart raced. To send or not to send. Another knock. He had to decide. He sent it, throwing the PD on the couch to answer the door.

His security camera revealed Wendy, Miranda and Merlin waiting.

'Here's that attention you ordered, sir.' Merlin spruiked as Kris opened up.

'Saxon told us the news,' Wendy said. 'You're taking Kurt and fucking off to Sydney to be a bigshot.' She pushed past Kris. 'I'll be managing the Lucid division.'

The other two followed her carrying beer and pizza. 'I got Sterling's job running uDream,' Merlin added. 'Now it's time to gorge like a tick on a calf.'

Kris smiled to himself. 'Come on in.' He went to close the door.

Merlin stopped. 'Don't close it, Kurt and Russell just pulled up.'

Chapter Twelve

Cosmos pink clouds reflected off majestic buildings as Merlin, Liam, Arrow and Zen boarded the vehicle. Their craft ascended five meters and then accelerated towards the bridge in the distance.

'The last round of rendering has made an impressive difference to the overall aesthetic of the city, Liam, it looks great,' Merlin commented.

'It has,' Liam agreed. 'The new colour palette of blues and pinks gives it a more welcoming feel.'

'I like the colours, but my favourite thing will always be Colossus,' Zen gushed. One red, a green and a blue building each resembling an ancient Egyptian statue, reached 1000 metres into the sky. They faced one another, their arms outstretched and joined, creating a circle. Colossus dominated the Pryma cityscape. 'They are so cool! Are we heading for the Signet 3 again?'

'Not this time, we're going to explore Colossus,' Arrow announced with a smile.

'Fuck yeah! Yes! Yes! Yes! Yes! Yes!'

Liam rolled his eyes. 'You are a loud girl, Zen.'

Arrow laughed. 'We're going to walk through the circle arms and visit the viewing platform in the headdress at the top of the red building.'

'Excellent!' Zen squealed as the craft landed in the drop-off zone in front of the green building.

The interior foyer was classic 23rd century design, random shapes with a hint of alien; the wall rendering resembled the cross section of an ant nest. A cylindrical water wall standing 50 metres was the central focal point, skirted by an impressive rainforest garden. People ate at cafés and milled around a Signet 1 & 2 exhibit.

The group strolled around the spacious centre, window shopping, checking out the latest in space fashion.

'I want those boots,' Arrow said as Zen joined her at the store window. 'Aren't they gaudy?'

'Very,' Zen agreed. 'I dream about boots like that.'

'Do elevated echoes dream?' Liam blurted.

Both Merlin and Arrow turned to Liam.

'What's an elevated echo?' Zen asked.

'I'll tell you about it later,' Merlin told her.

'Why don't you try out the credit system and buy those boots?' Liam insisted, redirecting the conversation.

The girls entered the store.

'Sorry about that, it just came out,' Liam apologised.

'They don't fucking dream, they can't,' Merlin snapped.

'Understood.'

A long pause filled the space between them as they wandered over to check out the Signet missions exhibit.

'So, this is the final design stage for Pryma, the setting of the backstory,' Merlin said.

'Yes. As Pryma is the jumping off point here on Makemake, users now have the option to explore the city or take the shuttle straight to the galactic fleet station,' Liam explained. 'I've been busting my balls to get this done for The Event.'

'Maybe we shouldn't have shown Saxon, then he wouldn't have pushed to have stage one finished for the launch. The awesome foursome are just too fucking talented,' Merlin grinned. 'You've done a phenomenal job pulling this project together in three months, Liam, it was a big ask.'

'Once we nailed the storyboard, it was just a matter of letting the imagination run wild.'

'I love Wendy's latest space yacht design for the galactic vessels,' Merlin chatted.

'The first and second versions were good, but the final version is inspired. It's outside the box.'

Merlin turned his attention back to the exhibit. 'The beacon was detected but they couldn't work out what it did and who constructed it, right?'

'Sort of,' Liam said somewhat annoyed. He had explained the backstory for GalNexus to Merlin several times. 'In 2443, the signal was detected, so Signet 1 was sent to investigate but was lost, never found. In 2448, Captain Garro and her crew were dispatched in the Signet 2. They found the source of the signal here on Makemake, this dwarf planet at the outer edges of our Solar system. The beacon emitted a pulse pointing outside our system which Garro followed, finding GalNexus. This is a replica of the beacon.'

The tree-trunk-shaped object, uneven, rough and gnarled, shimmered white. A multitude of constantly moving pearlescent tentacles emerging from the top of the trunk seemed to be feeling, sensing, interpreting its surroundings. One feeler touched Merlin's face and he pulled away. The beacon changed colour to red, its antenna retracting.

'Is it alive?' Merlin asked. 'It reminds me of a ginormous sea anemone.'

'It is alive. It's a species called Vig. Their spores travel on the galactic winds, dispersing throughout our galaxy like a weed. Once imbedded, Vig remain stationary throughout their 10,000-year life. They can be trained to repeat a continuous harmonic signal or pulse, so they're used as signposts for space travellers.'

'You realise we'll need a follow-on to GalNexus. Once people have experienced it, invested time in it, they'll crave a bigger, bolder adventure.'

'Already working on it. Time Trek Wars,' Liam announced with a cheeky grin. 'It develops from within the GalNexus storyline between the–'

'Check these out!' Arrow interrupted, prancing around in purple knee-high boots.

'Aren't they rad!' Zen squealed. 'Arrow bought me a pair too.' They joined arms and marched in step in a circle.

'Stonking boots, girls,' Merlin complemented.

'Let's test them out,' Liam said. 'We have a couple of kilometres to walk up on circle level.'

'Let's go!' Zen gushed.

Gentle December snow fell on New York City as it woke on Friday 13th.

'Remember what happened to Larry Page?' A woman asked her male companion as they walked behind their dog.

Saxon listened to the pair as his luggage was being unloaded from the vehicle onto the porterbot.

'Larry Page?' The man queried.

'Co-founder of Google,' the woman explained.

'Oh, Larry Page, yeah. No, I wouldn't wish that on anyone.'

The foyer of the upmarket hotel and apartment building was ornate, even opulent.

A young female concierge greeted Saxon with a warm smile. 'Welcome back, Dr Zynn.'

'Thank you,' Saxon replied, remembering his two-man security detail. 'Can we get these men a key?'

'Of course, Dr Zynn. Active for...?'

'Three days.'

The woman typed on her tablet. 'Place your PDs on the tablet please gentlemen,' she directed. 'Good. Set to go. Your apartment was serviced and stocked yesterday. Will there be anything else, Dr Zynn?'

'Refresh my memory. The new gym is on level 34, right?

'Thirty-second floor, Dr Zynn.'

'Correct. Yes, yes it used to be on 34. Thank you.'

The porterbot followed the trio into the elevator.

'30th floor,' Saxon told the elevator as his PD buzzed.

'You there yet?' Margo asked.

'Just going up to the apartment now. You in bed?'

'Getting there, it's 11:15 here. Morning for you.'

'Just gone 7:15. I'm going to hit the gym before brekkie.'

'Did you sleep on the plane?'

'Yep. I stole a couple of your zolpidem.'

'We've presold 17.7 million units,' Margo announced.

'Shit, that's great! A quarter of inventory.'

'Pretty much. We had a couple of problems today. Our social data miners in Sydney picked up chatter about counterfeit DI units in China. Firerock deployed teams and raided three factories along with local authorities and destroyed 680,000 units.'

'Did they carry quantum ID?'

'They did, but incorrect ID's.'

'We need Firerock to pursue the fucking Chinese ringleaders and send them a message,' Saxon proposed. 'Their cheap and nasty components could kill someone.'

'We will.' Margo yawned. 'There's been a hiccup in the entertainment line-up too.'

'What now?'

'Tamsin's manager pulled her out this morning; she's come down with a serious throat infection,' Margo explained. 'Lucky for us Selma's husband is an audio engineer at the studio where Jed Gentry's recording in Sydney, and Jed has agreed to step in.'

'Is that good?'

'That's great. Jed is more popular than Tamsin. MDV3 will still play New York and Qrawl in London. This line-up will boost our ratings.'

'Plus the holoshow,' Saxon said, 'It will blow people away.'

'It should.' Margo yawned again. 'It's been a big day, I'm trashed. I'm going to bed.'

'Good luck tomorrow.'

'And you this afternoon. I'll be glad when this is all over and we can get back to business as usual.'

'Is there a usual?' Saxon suggested.

'I guess not. Love you.' Margo disconnected.

On the 30th floor of the Fifth Avenue complex, one of Saxon's bodyguards held his PD against the door near the handle to unlock apartment 3002. Saxon waited while the security men did a sweep of the sparsely decorated, stylish apartment. Given the all clear, the porterbot obediently entered and began to remove luggage from its rack.

Meanwhile in London, at the Dorchester's Trellis restaurant, Kris finished his lunch before heading up to their suite on the ninth floor.

Nikola sat up in bed watching the wall screen. The Event countdown banner on London's News 24 channel read, 7 hours 40 minutes.

'So, tell us, Reggie, what can we expect from the long-anticipated Event tonight?' Stark Green, TV personality, asked his guest.

'The three-hour event will go live simultaneously from three locations around the world. Sydney, starting at 7:00 am local time, New York at 3:00 pm, and here in London at 8:00 pm tonight. There will be six segments, three music sets and three holoshows, each 30 minutes. Qrawl will kick the show off in London and they'll be projected onto the stages in Sydney and New York, with an estimated world viewing audience of five billion plus. They'll be followed by a holoshow, replicated in all three indoor arenas. Jed Gentry and his band will then play live from Sydney—'

'Hold on. Jed Gentry?' Stark interrupted. 'I thought Tamsin was playing in Sydney?'

'Tamsin has unfortunately called in sick, and Jed has come to the party.'

'Bad luck Tams,' Stark teased.

Reggie continued. 'There will be another 30-minute holoshow before MDV3 play for half an hour from New York, followed by the final holoshow ending with the Dream Immersion Platform going live.'

'So these holoshows and projected bands, what's new about it, Reg?' Stark asked.

'This will be our first look at the new ILM Holo-array. Word has it the ILM Holo-array is a game changer in holoprojection and how it works is a closely guarded secret. It synchronises 248 holo-transmitters deployed around each arena, concentrating a single focal point with such precision, it creates what appears to be solid 3D images. Add ultrasonic holographic sound and the Holo-array will bring to life one act performing live in three locations. But we're told the truly remarkable features of the Holo-array will excel when it premieres 20 dream immersion scenes selected from the 1200 Lucid titles soon to be on offer to users. While all this is going on centre stage, 100 lucky spectators at each venue will be randomly chosen every 30 minutes to enjoy dream immersion in a pop-up Dreamplex.'

'Sounds massive, Reggie, and Tristan Grazer, the action megastar, will be hosting The Event from London.'

'Yes, Stark. Tristan will be the face of The Event and I'm sure front and centre at many sponsor after parties.'

Kris entered the palatial hotel suite. 'How are you feeling?' He asked as he sidled up to Nikola on the king size bed.

She muted the screen. 'Better. I had a sleep. I'm still not hungry. I'm determined to be at the launch tonight. I didn't fly halfway around the world to stay in bed. How did your meeting go?'

'The building seems big enough, location is good, but it's old. The power supply needs to be upgraded. We'll sign a five-year lease if the owner pays half the upgrade costs. If they come to the party, the London DI Academy location is sorted.'

'It's exciting.'

'That it is. Fingers crossed, Saxon will sign off on the New York location and then we'll travel between here, New York and Sydney for the next few years.'

Nikola lent in to kiss Kris but stopped short. 'Sorry, I forgot. I don't want you to get this bug.'

'No thank you. Did you hear about Tamsin?'

'Yeah, fucking shame. She was the only act I really wanted to see.'

Kris' PD buzzed. He walked over and read the text. 'Fuck it. What is it with power today? Now there's an issue with power at the arena. I'll need to go and sort it. Get some more sleep, I want you there tonight.' He blew her a kiss as he left.

Eight hours later, Saxon surveyed the sold-out New York arena from his VIP box. Qrawl mesmerised the twenty thousand spectators cheering, unequivocally buying into the illusion centre stage.

Multiple large screens displayed similar crowd scenes in Sydney and London as euphoria intoxicated the entire planet collectively celebrating the dream immersion phenomenon. Vision of Walt, Kris and Nikola in London popped onto one screen, while on another, Margo could be seen engaged in conversation with Kurt in Sydney.

Saxon typed, *Is this heaven?* into his PD. The message went to Margo. Saxon watched Margo on the arena screen as she received the text. She smiled.

No, this is our reality! Enjoy! The text came back.

Makeup artists completed the final touches to Saxon and the host's makeup as an eager floor manager cleared the set. 'Ten seconds,' she said.

Talk show personality, Ivy Lane, cleared her throat. 'Ready, Dr Zynn?'

Saxon smiled and nodded.

'Live in five, four,' the floor manager continued the countdown with her fingers.

'Welcome back. As promised, the dream master, Dr Saxon Zynn, inventor of the Dream Immersion Platform is with us on this historic evening. Welcome, Dr Zynn.'

'Glad to be here, Ivy.'

'You have published over two dozen peer reviewed, and highly regarded papers, on neurochemistry during your time at Oxford, and now you've created a technology that has spawned social contagion around the world. How would you say your career is progressing?' The New Yorker asked.

Saxon grinned at her satire. 'I'm making a living. No, honestly, I've been an extremely fortunate man, surrounded by people who have supported me, believed in my ideas. The achievement of dream immersion has always been a team effort over many years.'

'Following this afternoon's enormously successful launch with stunning visuals from the ILM Holo-array, and sales exceeding your projections, where does ZynnComm go from here?'

'We continue to develop the company, by improving our products and expanding our three divisions. Lucid is rapidly growing our catalogue of retail experiences. Our custom personal experiences division, uDream, is surpassing all our expectations. Our Dream Stream division is working tirelessly with governments and business to produce training and corporate experiences. We are partnering with existing and new media companies to develop their own dream networks. We've opened our Dream Immersion Academy in Sydney, training the next generation of developers, and I can announce tonight, we'll be opening an Academy here in New York, and another in London in the next few months.'

'When will the Gatekeeper of Dream units come to market for start-ups wanting to produce their own content?'

'We've distributed about 190 advance units to our partners, so they can test the tech, but the general release will be in April next year.'

'One of those partners is Acid Spear Studios, financed by Michael Santoro under the direction of Sterling Lindquist, one of your ex-employees. They're the creator of the Sinnerverse network, a network hyped as the darkest corner of your mind. Have you ventured into Sinnerverse, Dr Zynn?'

'No, no I haven't.'

'One of my researchers has and said it was horrific. When you were developing dream immersion, did you ever envisage it being used this way?'

'Ivy, anything is possible in dream immersion, that's the beauty of the technology. How adults choose to develop it, choose to engage with it, is up to them.'

'There is already talk in some countries of banning the Sinnerverse network. Would you agree with that, Dr Zynn?'

'No, no I would not. Prohibition of any kind has never worked, be it drugs, books, alcohol or pornography. Prohibition simply drives it underground and criminal elements exploit it to get rich. Human beings, adult human beings, should have the choice to participate, or not, at their own discretion. I don't believe governments should have the power to say to any individual, no, you can't use that technology. Freedom of choice is a fundamental individual human right. If you think Sinnerverse might offend or terrify you, simply stay away. ZynnComm has plenty of experiences that will entertain the mainstream public for years.'

'It has been reported the Korean company HBU Electronics is close to developing a product similar to dream immersion. Have you been keeping an eye on your competition?'

'No, Ivy, but I'm sure competitors will try to develop similar technology. What worries me are the counterfeiters, those producing bogus dream immersion products that could potentially kill users. All our products are quality assured before being sold through reputable retailers. They carry our unique quantum ID code. Anyone considering buying dream immersion equipment should only buy from authorised retailers, making sure they verify our quantum ID code using their PD's at point of sale.'

'I've experienced dream phaze or dream immersion half a dozen times in the last few months; it's indistinguishable from reality. It is mindboggling tech you've created–'

'Thank you. It took years of trial and error, believe me.'

'I would imagine dream immersion could become quite addictive. Do you expect certain types will abuse the technology?'

'That is exactly why we've limited the use of dream immersion on several fronts. We've worked diligently to put safeguards in place to prevent abuse. If you use DI as intended, once a day, that is fine, but some people will try to misuse it. The dashboard only allows one experience per 24 hours per individual, and the Norus network time stamps users DNA to check and ensure that is the case. Thalpherycine dispensers issue one wafer per person per 24 hours. If the web enabled dispensers are tampered with the security mechanism renders the whole batch unusable. Without thalpherycine present, the dashboard won't work and dream immersion can't happen. Bottom line is, Ivy, there are checks and balances, the platform works in concert, remove one element and it doesn't happen.'

The Razorbacks were struggling amid the roar from the assembled crowd. Merlin, Zen, Arrow, Wendy, Miranda and Liam, dressed in red jumpsuits, had one measly point on the scoreboard against the Mad Monks from Malaysia. The drivers, Kurt, Kris and Michael, Wendy's brother, had allowed their opponents to press the yellow button atop the red obelisk three times before the changeover.

Hand signals and gestures practised in training were the only communication methods open to the dodgers. Calls and whistles had been abandoned because audience noise drowned out any verbal comms. Merlin signalled to Arrow and Liam; he would act as decoy for the driver defending the ramp. From three different directions, Merlin, Arrow and Liam ran towards the lone defender. The driver sat confused. A second defender was on the way. Merlin's bonus weapon was a slingshot with a bag of steel marbles. He began firing at the first driver's helmet, grabbing their attention. Arrow and Liam ran towards the ramp. Scampering up the incline, Liam got to the obelisk first and turned his back to it, leaning against it. The second defender accelerated up the ramp forcing Arrow to jump out of its path. Liam circled the obelisk as the defender tried to force him off the platform. Running at speed, Arrow's right foot found the back of the vehicle, allowing her to step across onto Liam's back then shoulders. He stood tall. She made it to the middle of the obelisk grappling for the best hand and foot holes. The audience willed her higher and higher. Finally, she reached out smashing the yellow button, activating the siren and flashing lights, releasing confetti bubbles into the crowd. The arena went berserk.

Frustrated, the Mad Monk driver accelerated directly at Liam who sidestepped at the last moment. The driver adjusted course, clipping the obelisk, immediately incurring a foul and a point deducted from the Mad Monks. The scores were now tied with two minutes to go.

Zen ran towards a narrow obstacle closely followed by a defender. She jumped, planting her hands dead centre of the rectangular top, somersaulting onto her feet. Zen signalled to Wendy to get ready for an assault. Distracted, Wendy was attacked from behind by a driver, smashing her into a metal post, crushing her spine and splitting open her belly. The blood thirsty mass cheered, applauding the strategy.

Miranda paused, looking across at her partner's twisted body sprawled on the blood- soaked ground. She couldn't linger, because the same driver was now gunning for her. Her foe drove straight at her, but Miranda stood her ground. At the last moment, she sprang high into the air, twisting, coming down behind the vehicle. The vehicle stopped dead then reversed. Miranda jumped onto the pod. She crawled up behind the driver and pulled at their helmet, choking the driver. The driver unlatched their helmet with one hand. Miranda yanked off the helmet and began whacking the female driver repeatedly in the head with the helmet. The defender released the joystick, protecting her head with her arms. Miranda continued to pound the woman, forcing the driver to unfasten her five-point harness and jump from the pod, disqualifying her from the game. Miranda felt the adrenaline pulsating through her body as Merlin signalled to rally for an attack on the obelisk.

Five dodgers, two defenders, one minute remained.

'Let's settle for a draw,' Liam suggested to Merlin.

'Not this little black duck,' came his response.

'What?' Liam asked.

Merlin looked at him. 'Don't worry about it. Let's go with the jumpstart play.'

'That's the raised platform play, right?' Liam asked.

'It is. This one's for Wendy.'

The Christmas lunch barbecue at Margo and Saxon's Sydney home was a relatively quiet affair for the tight-knit group. Their beautifully landscaped waterfront backyard was prime real estate on one of the most iconic waterways in the world. Merlin and Arrow explored the harbour close to shore on water-walkers while Wendy, Kurt's carer Russell, Selma and her husband, Granger, Miranda and Nikola sat around the table in the impressive poolside cabana, talking and grazing on an assortment of delectable nibbles.

Saxon deftly managed the barbecue with beer in one hand and tongs in the other, flipping, manoeuvring and generally prodding the sausages, steak and chicken. Swigging his beer, Kurt supervised.

'Ready for these?' Kris delivered the onions from the kitchen.

'Sure.' Saxon quickly cleared a space on the hotplate. 'There you go.'

The oil doused onions sizzled and spat as Kris emptied them onto the barbecue. 'I received an email from one of our star codesters at the Academy this morning. He's leaving, he's been headhunted.'

'Who?' Saxon asked.

'Hadrian Judge.'

'The young man who lost his parents in the Gambaldi incident?'

'Yeah. He said a corporate recruitment company called Aspen and Young have been sniffing around student drinking holes,' Kris explained. 'They're recruiting for Amanda Voss.'

'Fundamental Purists?'

'They want to elevate Jeremy Abernathy in dream immersion. He'll rise from the dead to continue to preach the word to his followers.'

Saxon laughed. 'Of course he will. Fucking hypocrites. Was Hadrian a trainee?'

'No, paying student,' Kurt answered.

'I called him,' Kris continued. 'He was very apologetic. The kid is smart, really smart. Fast-tracked through training. I offered him a position, but he said they were offering triple the money.'

'We train and they continue to drain our talent pool,' Saxon said.

'We've been thinking about the trainee program,' Kris said, glancing at Kurt. 'We need to change our Academy model to reflect the new job sector we're developing. We think a two tiered paradigm. The second being a blending of an indentured apprentice and a military contract. We need to strengthen our contract beyond training, to ensure we get ROI from them,' Kris suggested.

'I agree,' Saxon said, before finishing off his beer.

'Tier one would be our fee paying bread and butter students studying the six-month FH code Cadet Certificate,' Kurt jumped in enthusiastically. 'The second tier will be our Academy Dream Team program. They start as Cadet Codesters for the first six-months, same as paying students, then progress as Content Codesters for 18 months back at the facility, cutting their teeth on basic element design and narrative. At the end of that 24 months they graduate as Dream Developer First Class. Dream Developer Major would require a further 12 months of commitment and experience, and finally another 12 months to achieve Dream Master status.'

'That sounds very structured...quite regimented,' Saxon said. 'Trainees were relevant when we had no competition I suppose. What do we do if they break the contract? What are the consequences?'

'Okay, so trainee contracts would disappear. Dream Team contracts start at a minimum 24 months. We offer cadets a bonus once they finish their six month training and again once they reach the 24 month milestone of Dream Developer First Class.'

'And, if they piss off early?' Saxon pressed.

'We hunt them down and kill them.' They all laughed. 'Seriously, they can never re-enrol for further quals,' Kris said straight up. 'We are our own masters in this regard, we regulate the industry, we set the benchmarks and standards, we are the source of truth. Companies will want to start hiring qualified codesters, beginning with Cadet Certificate holders, or for price, a Dream Developer First Class, Major, or a Master. If Dream Team codesters quit ZynnComm to go elsewhere before their initial two-year contract is up, they end up walking away with only a Cadet Certificate, and put on a blacklist, never allowed to re-enrol at the Academy.'

'Harsh. I like it,' Saxon chortled.

'We make it clear to cadets from the get-go; we will commit to them but they must commit to us in return. We pay them to train, we employ them for 18 months, but there will be consequences if they leave before their two-year contract expires. If they wish to stay beyond the initial 24 months, we incentivise it accordingly with a sign-on bonus, medical cover and increased salary–'

Margo walked past from the kitchen. 'Come on you three. Enough shop talk. Let's eat.'

'Yes, ma'am,' Saxon responded with a casual salute. 'I like it.' He whispered. 'We'll catch up later,' he told the pair.

Merlin and Arrow arrived back at the marquee at the same time Saxon placed the meat on the table.

'You have an uncanny knack of turning up just as the food arrives, Merlin,' Wendy commented.

'Timing is everything,' he grinned. 'Like winning Obelisk yesterday with only two seconds on the clock. Puts a smile on my dial.'

As the sweltering day refused to end, Margo relaxed in the cabana reading a magazine.

Saxon stood staring at yachts, cast crimson by the setting sun, slicing glassy water, creating frothy white tracks across Sydney Harbour. He wandered back to his chair and beer. 'I've been thinking more about Hugo lately,' he confided.

Margo rested her magazine on her lap. 'Yeah, I've been feeling a little empty contemplating Christmas without him. This will be our first Christmas when we haven't all been together.' Margo reflected. 'We have all the money in the world, but what do we really have?'

Saxon sipped his beer. 'Have you spoken to Waylon recently?'

'Not since you got back from New York, so a few days.'

Saxon chuckled. 'Remember when we gave Hugo potatoes wrapped as a really cool present for his fifth birthday?'

'You did that, not me. It was cruel.'

'He was so excited. The look of disappointment on his face when he opened it. Priceless.'

'You made him cry. You have a sick sense of humour.'

'Just carrying on a tradition. My father gave me potatoes, and I gave Lena potatoes when she turned five.' Saxon paused for a moment. 'We gave him his first surfboard straight afterwards. He was happy.'

'Fucking stupid tradition.'

Saxon sipped his beer. 'Polish tradition that goes back to the end of the second world war–'

'Yeah I know, I know. That's all they had to give as presents.'

'It was all bullshit,' Saxon admitted with a wry smile. 'My fucking father made it up.'

'What? So why did you do it to Hugo?'

'I found out at Mum and Dad's funeral, years after Hugo's fifth birthday. Arthur Muntz, one of Dad's friends, told me he made it up as a joke. Laughed his guts out when I told him about the tradition. I thought I told you this?'

'Nope.' Margo's PD buzzed. 'Guess who.'

'Walt.'

'How did you know that?'

'He messaged me yesterday and said he would be calling with a business proposition.'

Margo tapped her PD to project Walt's image. 'Hi, Dad.'

'You in holiday mode?'

'Of course. Not long finished a barbecue with a few of the work crew. You?'

'Not quite, I'll be back in Sydney next week. Is Saxon with you?'

Margo turned her PD. 'Yes.'

'Hi, Walt,' Saxon greeted as he joined Margo.

'My PD has been running hot since The Event. People want to buy ZynnComm.'

'Not for sale, Walt,' Saxon told him.

'I thought so too, Saxon, until I got a call from Lee Jung-Lee. He made me an offer I'm finding hard to resist.'

'HBU Electronics?' Saxon questioned. 'I thought they were working on their own version of our tech?'

'I asked him about that. Seems they're several years away. He wants ours now.'

'It's not for sale, Dad,' Margo reconfirmed.

'Jung-Lee offered 612 billion US for Tremaine's 49.2 percent.'

'Shit!' Margo exclaimed.

'Saxon, he is willing to go to 624 billion for your share,' Walt baited.

Margo and Saxon stared at each other.

'You know money has never been my motivation, Walt,' Saxon explained. 'Do you really need more money?'

'It's fucking business, Saxon. We are in business to make money. Only one Jung-Lee comes along in a lifetime.'

'Are you planning on selling the Tremaine Group stock, Dad?' Margo asked, holding her breath.

'I'm meeting with the board tomorrow afternoon to seriously consider it.'

'We won't be selling, Walt, whatever the board decides,' Saxon informed him. 'Imagine our value once the Gatekeeper of Dreams is released and we're the backbone of all content development.'

'We'll weigh up all options. As we speak, I've got the bean counters developing short and medium term projections based on sales in recent days,' Walt advised. 'We won't make a decision lightly.'

'This could be chaotic for us if Jung-Lee wants to disrupt operations to force us to sell,' Margo proposed.

'The ancient Greeks thought chaos was the origin of everything, the first thing that ever existed, out of which everything was created–'

'Fuck off with your philosophical bullshit! Is this out of spite, Dad? Because we kept you out of the loop for the past few months?'

'Not at all. This is business.' He disconnected.

'Fucking old bastard,' Margo scoffed. 'Why would he even entertain the proposition?'

'Puts us in an awkward position if he sells.'

They contemplated the possibility of working with an unfamiliar partner. Being hamstrung by decision making processes that could be fraught with endless meetings and negotiations regarding the simplest of operational matters.

'This could totally fuck up our holidays if he does,' Margo declared.

'Correct.'

The wall screen was muted when Saxon passed by the living room next morning on his way from the bedroom to kitchen. A glimpse of Amanda Voss piqued his interest. 'Unmute screen,' he instructed the house assistant.

'Jeremy was a staunch opponent of dream immersion technology, he did everything in his power to warn people,' Amanda defended. 'Time will tell what the long term ramifications of this technology will be. But now, the genie is out of the bottle and we can't put it back. We've decided to grab this genie by the balls.'

'Of course you will Amanda,' Saxon muttered.

'How do you plan on using dream immersion?' The interviewer asked.

'We are creating the Fundamental Purists network. In dream immersion Jeremy will be elevated to regain his position as the spiritual leader of the Fundamental Purists. He will deliver a daily sermon to guide and support our congregation as he did when he was with us.'

'Don't you think that's hypocritical given your husband's stance? Wouldn't he object to becoming part of the dream phaze culture?'

Amanda didn't answer straight away. 'Jeremy Abernathy was a complex man–'

Margo entered the room and stood beside Saxon. 'Isn't that Amanda Voss?'

'Yep.'

'Is she blasting us again?'

'Just the opposite,' Saxon said. 'She's starting her own DI network, elevating Jeremy so he can preach to his sheep.'

'N0000. Fucking charlatan. She battled us for years, now she's going to embrace it for financial benefit.'

'She shits ice cubes this woman.'

'Do you think...we could elevate Hugo?' Margo asked quietly.

Saxon looked at her. 'Mute screen,' he ordered. 'You think he's dead?'

Margo played with her fingernails. 'I don't think so...but I really miss him.'

Saxon took her hands in his. 'I do too, but I don't think he's dead.'

'Waylon can't find him.'

'He's off the network. He's gone to ground on purpose so we can't find him. He's not stupid.'

'I hope so.' Margo's PD buzzed in her pocket. She took it out and glanced at the caller ID. 'It's Waylon. Should I answer it?'

'Bring his projection up,' Saxon told her.

'Hi, Margo. I have good news.' Waylon said. 'We've found Hugo.'

'Where?'

'He's working in a Darwin café called Mermaid's Lagoon, going by the name Charlie Dodgson.'

Saxon wrapped his arm around Margo as tears welled in her eyes. 'That's not good news, that's fucking great news, Waylon! Thank you. Is he okay?'

'He seems fine. He's sharing a house near the beach. Works five days a week as a kitchenhand. He has a crewcut and beard now, with a few earrings.'

'Is he coming home for Christmas?' Saxon asked.

'There's been no contact with him, only surveillance at this stage.'

'When are you going to approach him?' Margo asked eagerly.

'Just hear me out,' Waylon offered. 'I'm not sure we should. He's safe, he's earning a living, and he's not the son of the most famous power couple on the planet at the moment. You might like to keep it that way until he reconciles in his own mind what he wants to do.'

Margo and Saxon weighed up Waylon's reasoning.

'Have you got photos of him?' Margo asked. A moment later, images of a transformed Hugo appeared on Margo's PD screen. 'He looks...healthy...happy...so...grown up.'

'I think you're right, Waylon,' Saxon agreed. 'Let him be. We know he's safe. You'll keep an eye on him?'

'Of course. He's on our radar and I'll keep you posted.'

'Thank you, Waylon, for the best Christmas present ever,' Margo said. 'We hope you and your family have a wonderful holiday break.'

'I will. I received the DI dashboards you sent, thanks. My eldest boys and I will be doing some adventuring over the holidays.'

'Let me know if you need more, for your staff,' Saxon added.

'Thank you. Merry Christmas.' Waylon disconnected.

Saxon and Margo embraced as Margo sobbed with relief.

'Well, you never know what's coming do you?' Margo asked wiping her eyes.

'Not when it involves our Hugo,' Saxon replied. 'Should we fly to Darwin and stalk him from afar?' he jested, half serious.

Margo considered his suggestion. 'No...no. Maybe we should sell to Jung-Lee?'

'No. I like my idea better.'

'Should we try and convince my father not to sell?'

'Do you honestly think he'll listen to us?'

'No. Fuck it...we're on holidays, let's dream phaze.'

Dream Phaze Glossary

BASE - Bergman Analysis and Synthesis Engine. Gatekeeper of Dreams authored experiences are translated through a BASE neural compiler into Synmem code.

Biosoftware – neurochemical sequence that contains markers that 'express" in the presence of a biological activation code.

Black Shield – intuitive firewall protecting the Norus network.

Codesters – developers/programmers who write FH code and author dream immersion experiences.

Dream Immersion (DI) dashboard – interface worn on the forearm to access dream immersion. User selects experience preferences, and it initiates and monitors all stages of dream immersion. Translates Synmem code into inaudible frequencies and delivers them to earstims.

Dream immersion experiences – Once only Experience (OoE), a Series of Experiences (SoE) or a Continuing Experience (CE). This choice must be made prior to dream immersion.

Dreamforming – interface for authoring dream immersion experiences using a conception space and tool menu generated by Gatekeeper of Dreams hardware.

Dream Immersion Platform – technology created by Saxon Zynn for dream immersion experiences. Consists of five parts – dashboard, earstims, thalpherycine, Synmem code and the Norus network.

Dream Phaze – term meaning an 'engineered dream' rather than an organic, natural dream.

Dreamplex – mass dream immersion complex similar to a cinema complex.

Dynamic Emission Neuroimaging – is the use of several combined techniques to directly image neurotransmissions of the brain in real time.

Earfonic – single ear hook Bluetooth earphone with mic.

Earstims – delivers inaudible frequencies from the DI dashboard into the brain which sparks neurotransmitter chemical sequences in the thalamus. Thalpherycine must be present for Synmem code synthesis to take place.

Echoes - characters who populate dream immersion experiences.

Ø Live echoes are active users, living people

Ø Assembled echoes are the extras in every experience, they are created from scratch and populate all DI environments

Ø Elevated echoes are deceased people authored for specific experiences

Ø Host echoes can be live, elevated, or assembled characters. Hosts can be active across multiple experiences.

Exteroceptive - stimuli outside the body.

FH code – Frequency Hypgenic source code developed by Saxon Zynn for the Gatekeeper of Dreams engine which creates the tools and content for the dreamforming interface to author dream immersion experiences.

Firerock – Risk management organisation specialising in covert activities.

Fundamental Purists – Religious movement founded by Jeremy Abernathy.

Gatekeeper of Dreams – Hardware/engine used to author dream immersion experiences via the dreamforming interface, which converts the authored dream into Synmem code.

Gelchips – capable of carrying out 198 quintillion calculations per second.

Group consciousness integration matrix – software allowing users to be aware of and interact with other users within the dream immersion environment.

Haptic spontaneity - sense of touch; tactile freedom.

Interoceptive - stimuli arising within the body based on deep feeling and emotional reactions rather than on reason or thought.

Jazper - network intelligence and connectivity management system for the Norus network

Neuroelectrodynamics – study of the dynamics and interaction of electrical signals in the brain.

Neuroinformatics – combines data across all levels of neuroscience in order to understand brain function by the application of computational models and analytical tools.

Neuromorphic computing - software systems that implement models of neural systems mimicking neurobiological architecture.

Neurotransmission – the process of communication between two nerve cells.

Norus Network – dedicated computer network which facilitates and coordinates the entire Dream Immersion Platform.

Nukoin - popular digital currency.

MMDG – massive multiplayer dream game

Occipital lobe - the rearmost lobe in each cerebral hemisphere of the brain.

Personal Device (PD) – Universal device that people carry for communication, identity, GPS identifier, finances, medical, entertainment, analytical applications, workplace applications, security, and many other functions.

Pons - the part of the brain stem that links the medulla oblongata and the thalamus.

RIP bullet - Radically Invasive Projectile developed in the early 21st century.

Sense8 - predictive modelling engine used by developers for authoring 'echoes'. Part of Gatekeeper of Dreams suite of tools.

Spatial perception - the ability to be aware of your physicality within the environment around you.

Synapse - a junction between two nerve cells, consisting of a minute gap across which impulses pass by diffusion of a neurotransmitter. Also known as a neuronal junction.

Synaptic vesicles - In a nerve cell, synaptic vesicles store various neurotransmitters that are released at the synapse. The release is regulated by a voltage-dependent calcium channel. Vesicles are essential for propagating nerve impulses between nerve cells and are constantly recreated by the cell.

Synmem code – Synaptic memory neural code/software developed by Saxon Zynn for authoring neurochemical sequencing for dream immersion.

Thalpherycine – biosoftware activated by Synmem code, which works on several levels to create authored dreams using neurochemical sequencing.

Vectigon metrics - neurochemical behaviour modification.

Dream Phaze
https://www.dreamphaze.com/
hello@dreamphaze.com
Next novel in the Dream Phaze series:
Dream Phaze – Imagination (Book 2)

Don't miss out!

Visit the website below and you can sign up to receive emails whenever Matt Watters publishes a new book. There's no charge and no obligation.

https://books2read.com/r/B-A-RNPH-TWJY

BOOKS 2 READ

Connecting independent readers to independent writers.